TREASURE
And
BLOOD
The Legend of a Pirate

Tyla Cassidy-Raghunath

INTRODUCTION

Black Pirates and the Tale of Henri Caesar

I've always been fascinated by the intriguing, controversial and deeply murky world of piracy.

During the Golden Age of Piracy which spanned from 1650 to 1726, bands of marauding pirates threatened and menaced commercial and sometimes even military shipping in the Caribbean, along the North American eastern seaboard, the West African coast and the Indian Ocean.

A pirate ship was once one of the few places a black man could possibly attain power, money and, ironically, respectability in the Western Hemisphere. Many of these black pirates were, in fact, fugitive slaves in the Caribbean or other coastal areas of the Americas. Others joined pirate crews when their slave ships or plantations were raided. Consequently, it was a simple choice between a state of perpetual unrelenting slavery or emancipation through lawlessness and criminality.

Apparently, approximately one third of the 10,000

pirates recorded during the Golden Age of Piracy were former slaves and these included women and frequently orphaned or abandoned children. I'm under no illusion that many were severely mistreated on the pirate ships and compelled to carry out the lowest subservient duties. Some exceptional pirate captains established revolutionary equality amongst the men, irrespective of race. On these particular ships black men could bear arms and enjoy an equal share of the plunder. I think, in contrast, it's crucial to note that when back on the mainland cruel injustice and stark consequences of slavery equally prevailed. Interestingly, white pirates were usually hanged when apprehended but their black counterparts were often returned to their original owners or resold back into slavery; in my opinion, a fate far more painful than death itself.

My book focuses on one such black pirate named Henri Caesar who was active in the late 16th century. He was born into the noble family of a West African tribal chieftain but forced into a life of piracy at a young age. He became notorious for raiding ships in the Florida Keys and the Caribbean and became a consort for the infamous English pirate Blackbeard, otherwise known as Edward Teach, on his well-documented ship the *Queen Anne's Revenge*. As befitting for a true and authentic pirate, his life is shrouded in legend and mystery. He was thought to have been a large, formidable man, brutal and menacing yet still blessed with intelligence and ingenuity. His success as a much-feared pirate on the high seas meant that he quickly rose up the ranks in the murderous world that few could ever master. Consequently, he amassed an impressive fortune and gained the dubious reputation of a gentlemen thief, in fact, acquiring a perverse kind of respectability in his later years.

This is the story of Henri Caesar, an exceptional pirate, which is not a tale for the faint-hearted or the judgmental. It's simply an account of the complex life of a courageous man who survived against the odds; the ruthless but brave son of the heir to the Ashanti people of West Africa who became one of the most prolific and feared pirates in history.

CHAPTER 1

Beginning

A very long time ago, when fearless pirates ruled the turquoise oceans of the world, in the deepest, darkest depths of West Africa, the son and heir to the well-respected and prosperous tribal chief of the Ashanti people was born. The year was 1676. His name was Henri Caesar and it was rumoured in the village that, at the exact moment of the baby prince's birth, the sky turned a peculiar shade of crimson and lightning bolts rained down relentlessly like razor-sharp swords sending the terrified blue swallow birds racing across the river; in fact, never to be seen again.

As the years passed the young heir showed great academic ability, becoming fluent in both his native African dialect and French, as well as showing an athletic prowess in sports and hunting well beyond his years. Caesar was much loved and cherished by his parents, Saul and Letitia, and because he was their only child he was very precious, like a shining diamond in their tribal royal crown.

Caesar's first memory was as a lively and exuberant five-year-old prince hunting with his father and uncle, Lesotu, in the treacherous outland for antelope and jaguar. The elders for the Ashanti were always amazed and impressed by this fearless child and surprised that, even on his first kill, he wanted to cut the throat of the prey. His mother loved to recount the story: she would say that her son was mesmerised as, after cutting the prey's throat, he would watch closely as the deep red blood cascaded into the garishly decorated hunting vessel. She knew that her son was already an unusual and determined young boy, advanced and hungry for both knowledge and recognition. These impressive attributes would develop and strengthen and, by the time Caesar was 15 years old, he was already a respected and revered young heir. As a consequence the villagers loved and cared for him immensely.

Caesar had just celebrated his birthday when, unexpectedly, his parents decided to visit the chief of the neighbouring Vestuku Island. The purpose of this trip was to unite their villages and islands to share information. It had been brought to their attention that a conspiracy by the arrival of a chief from another village on Fellanu Island was planning to invade and conquer all the West African villages, making their futures dangerous and very precarious.

Upon hearing this, the young Caesar felt a deep

feeling of trepidation about his parents' imminent voyage and begged them to take him along with them on the perilous trip. They refused as they were adamant he should stay at home to help his uncle Lesotu safeguard their village and build a fortress around the island. Finally relenting and reluctantly accepting his parents' decision, Caesar realised his worst fear. Deep down he knew his uncle was a devious and calculating snake and had always had the King's crown in his sights, but the King so trusted his younger brother, much to the dismay and frustration of Caesar. It was this stark realisation that sent fear and apprehension through his young mind. Only his resolve and courage would keep him alive on his island once his parents had departed. Caesar was brave and industrious beyond his years; after all, he was determined to survive and take his rightful place on the throne as the next King of Asante. Uncle Lesotu was no match for him; he would conquer and silence this evil pretender and, until his beloved parents returned, peace and prosperity would prevail.

On the day of his parents' departure Caesar felt deep sorrow and was consumed by an unnerving feeling of trepidation. His parents were his foundation and his world and he knew that it would be very difficult to deal with his sly and treacherous uncle. While Saul and Letitia had disappeared beyond the beautiful African sunset in the boat, very chillingly, Caesar suddenly noticed from the corner of his eye his uncle Lesotu's fixed gaze. He knew that this was a warning sign of impending doom and decided at that moment to reach deep inside himself for strength and fortitude. He would be on his guard every day – he knew his uncle would go to any lengths to destroy his spirit and was fully aware that from that day on his life was in grave danger.

Early next morning Caesar awoke and, aware that he was already missing his parents dreadfully, decided to spend some time in the comforting arms of the ocean. As he looked out beyond the vibrant amber glow of the horizon, he noticed that the soft turquoise waves clung over the jagged rocks; it felt quite hypnotic and was a comfort to him, an escape from his troubled young mind. H knew he needed to relax but the disturbing vision of his uncle's mean and villainous face played continuously like a perpetual nightmare. He could only depend on himself as the elders could be tempted by gold and would no doubt eventually swear allegiance to his cruel and wicked uncle. He was conscious it was only a matter of time before they would betray him.

Caesar felt the salty tears fall from his eyes. He missed his parents and their perpetual cloak of love and protection but, as he wiped the tears away, he remembered what his father had told him, to remember his blood was of royal lineage and that he could overcome any of life's obstacles. He had the protection of his ancestors and would always find a way to be victorious, with a brave and noble heart. With this realisation, Caesar felt strengthened and encouraged and resolved to do whatever it took to survive. He refused to let the menacing spectre of his uncle destroy his spirit and vowed to behave in the manner of a true king – strong, steadfast and always one step ahead in outsmarting his enemies. Lesotu would not covet his crown and he vowed to do whatever it took to protect his future and the safety of the villagers.

On the island the days turned into weeks and then months and, as a year passed, Caesar was losing all hope of ever seeing his beloved parents again. He was now 16 years of age and, according to Ashanti custom, could now be crowned King in his father's absence. Caesar had spoken to his father's trusted elder, Ejuki, and asked him if it was time for him to take over as King; he knew that it would have been his father's wish. Curiously, Ejuki didn't make eye contact with him and just said that the elders would seek the guidance and wisdom on this matter from Lesotu. Caesar knew instinctively that his original gut feeling was right – a conspiracy was being planned. Consequently, he would find out all he could for clearly nobody in the village could be trusted; a nest of vipers were conspiring but he resolved to defeat them – after all, he had no choice.

That evening, Lesotu summoned every village elder to a meeting. Upon realising this, Caesar decided to listen in covertly, using all his stealth and cunning to stay out of sight. With a very heavy heart he instinctively knew that they were conspiring to slay him in order to secure Lesotu as King and, with his parents' oblivious treachery in their absence, the young heir knew he must plan his imminent escape. Caesar crept like a sleek predatory panther towards Lesotu's house and, as he approached, he was struck by the vision of the vibrant sunset. Strokes of radiant pink and pale orange were etched into the African sky as if applied by an artist's hand.

Hiding out of plain sight and perched under a window, Caesar watched the treacherous Lesotu lead the six village elders into his house. Despite placing his life in grave danger by being so near he felt compelled to find out their true intentions and therefore plan his next move accordingly.

As he listened, his worst fears were confirmed. His ruthless uncle asked the six leaders in turn to accept that his brother and his wife would never be returning. He stressed that it had been a year since they set off on their perilous journey and since they had failed to return and sent no word back to the village it was assumed they had probably either perished at sea or been murdered. As the six men discussed the situation Lesotu suddenly announced that he would offer each loyal elder money, land and a higher tribal rank in exchange for their allegiance to make him King of Ashanti and that this would consequently mean that young Caesar would never sit on the throne. Five of the elders immediately agreed to this arrangement only thinking of their own ambition and avarice. Only Ejuki at first refused, asking Lesotu what would become of Caesar in his parents' absence, stressing that he was the rightful heir and that he wanted no part in his plan. Lesotu was furious at Ejuki's audacious refusal to comply and he pointed out that he would be committing treason by not agreeing and that, in fact, it was punishable by death. Realising that he had no choice but to agree to this despicable betrayal, Ejuki very reluctantly complied but felt so very guilty about being involved with this villainous plot.

As he crouched down in the pitch blackness, Caesar was deeply horrified by what had transpired and, realising that his life was in grave danger, he decided to escape from the island as soon as he could acquire a boat and supplies. He would live to fight another day – he was the true King of Ashanti – but for now he must stay safe. He would voyage to Vestuku Island in search of his absent parents, a quest he felt compelled to complete; the true spirit of the Ashanti would protect and guide him.

Caesar, realising the painful truth that he was to be murdered in cold blood and that the elders now fully understood they were under the evil influence of his despicable uncle, decided to leave at dawn. His escape would not be an easy undertaking but, by a stroke of sheer luck, Lesotu informed the elders that they would venture to the village's ceremonial compound that very hour to make a feast in celebration of his imminent coronation. Caesar waited till their shadowy figures disappeared and, once he was in Lesotu's house, he hastily grabbed an old hessian sack on the table and threw anything useful he could find into it: swords, a shield, rope, a hunting dagger and a fishing rod. He also raided the parlour for any food he could find. With a wry smile, Caesar made a hasty exit knowing that on discovering his boat, as well as the missing supplies, his uncle would be absolutely livid. Caesar felt justified and strengthened by his actions but he felt in no doubt that a subtle kind of revenge would play on his uncle's mind. Caesar was young but very bold and cunning like a young wolf hungry for blood, mustering enough courage to execute his plan.

Caesar dragged his bag of plunder to the shore and headed stealthily inside the strange grey granite cave he had played in as a young child. He planned to take the small wooden boat moored nearby in the black of night and make for his beloved Piku Island. His voyage to find his parents on Vestuku would be extremely perilous and inevitably fraught with danger, but he was prepared to endure any hardships in order to discover the whereabouts of his parents. He was an Ashanti warrior after all, imbued with steely resolve that would carry him over the crashing waves of the African ocean back into the arms of his beloved kin. And so, as dawn broke, Caesar quietly sailed away. His courage belied his tender years but he was exceptionally courageous and was determined to defeat any evil force that threatened his rightful place on the throne as the true King.

CHAPTER 2

The Voyage

As the days on the dangerous and unpredictable seas merged into weeks, the malnourished and weary Caesar wondered if he would ever sight land. One morning as the sunset emerged to beckon a new day, he noticed in the hazy distance the faint silhouette of a few towering palm trees. With a renewed sense of optimism and utilising all his youthful strength, the valiant boy powered the weather-beaten little vessel towards the shore. His determination to reach land was in full overdrive; his painfully scarred sunburnt hands now working the splintered oars at lightning speed. It seemed like an eternity until Caesar finally reach the shore. As he embarked, he felt both tentative and elated to have finally reached his destination. His flimsy wooden boat had disintegrated into pieces but he was very grateful that it had weathered this arduous journey. Exciting thoughts raced through his mind: *Which island is this? Is it indeed Vestuku Island? Will I finally be reunited with my parents?*

It occurred to Caesar that his worldly possessions were so depleted that he could carry them in both arms: a bundle of ragged clothes, a homemade fishing rod and, most importantly, the intricately carved jewellery box his mother had gifted him, which was a family heirloom passed down to the tribal chiefs. To Caesar it was his most treasured possession and it still contained the ornately beaded blue and yellow pendant symbolising the family colours – the fearsome Ashanti people of West Africa. It was a miracle that the ocean had not devoured this precious jewel and it was significant as it was the only memento of his true identity. He contemplated that, for now, he may well have fallen on hard times and been washed up on a strange and desolate island, but his lion-hearted prowess still beat with power and enduring pride.

The young heir was truly exhausted and depleted from his perilous journey across the menacing African ocean and, as he lay back on the carpet of dusty yellow sand, the last thing he remembered was the shrill cries of swooping gulls resonating in his ears. Caesar awoke to the searing and scorching rays of the sun and the endless abundance of fine white sand covering his aching and emaciated body like a delicate and temperamental blanket. It was jagged like a woven carpet of glass paper and due to the fact that he'd been lying on it all night it stung the skin on his

back like tiny red hot glowing coals. Fighting back the
pain he clambered to his feet, shaking off the endless
blankets of fine white sand. He realised that it was
imperative for his welfare and safety to construct an
encampment for himself. It would be a basic primitive
shelter, camouflaged and crucially covert to repel any
potential hostile and predatory islanders. He moved
with gazelle-like speed and had constructed a small
home which consisted of a ramshackle tent by sunset.
In fact, his old tarpaulin from the boat was propped
up precariously by random pieces of wood intertwined
with shiny green palm leaves. As he surveyed his
inventive handiwork the young boy prayed the island's
weather stayed consistently sunny and calm as any
unexpected storms or rain would reduce his new
shelter to a pile of despair – he would be propelled
back to the beginning, making no progress and finding
it difficult to keep motivated and positive in these very
stark, dangerous and challenging circumstances.

From the makeshift encampment that Caesar
now called his home he surveyed a vast expanse of
vivid blue and green that could be seen far into the
distance, like a breathtaking landscape painting. So
many thoughts filled his inquisitive young mind: *Are
there any humans lurking in the shadows? Am I on Netu
Island where my parents had headed in search of securing
supplies for their village all that time ago?* Caesar basked
in the swathe of green as he viewed his territory, a

tropical cascade of light and dark hues, dewy green leaves, green shrubs and long grass in the most unusual translucent bottle green and deep emerald green of the sea.

The island birds were many and consisted primarily of large, menacing creatures sweeping down in a steady stream at any time of day. Caesar thought their relentless presence could be interpreted as a dark and sinister omen of supernatural intent and, as their devilish black onyx eyes fixated upon him, he was convinced that they would have no hesitation in tearing his human flesh apart with their razor-sharp snapping beaks. He suddenly felt vulnerable and exposed and, despite his youthful bravado and steadfast courage, he was very inexperienced in the art of survival but nevertheless vowed to accept his present predicament and adapt accordingly. The sinister birds were of two very distinct varieties: one with garish yellow and blue glossy feathers of magnificent plumage, the other like an intricate tapestry of turquoise, translucent dove-white and pitch-black; when the sharp rays of sunlight descended on the flock the spectrum of beautifully-coloured feathers was revealed. Indeed, Caesar was in sheer awe of the island's rainbow of exotic and rare birds and their beauty was a welcome distraction in alleviating his loneliness and vulnerability. Caesar guessed that it was the summer of July 1693 and he wondered how the rest of the year would unfold.

The next morning a fierce torrent of rain showers pelted down mercilessly on the island like a never-ending stream of bullets on a fast-moving battlefield. As the heavens really opened Caesar noticed how it fell straight down onto the island, hammering down at 90° angles and forcing away the sand as it thundered down. It was only the fourth day on the mysterious and haunting island but the young prince had barely eaten and his body was depleted and weak. His lack of human companionship made him frequently apprehensive; he found the solitary life quite empty and, being so young and unsupported, it began to erode his already compromised natural survival instinct. His limited resources of nourishment, the bitter and ant-ridden leaves found on random bushes with the red berries scattered like random spots of blood on the green leaf carpet were not sustaining him. His only source of water was a small pond on the west side of his encampment which was a murky shade of green, tainted with frequent visits from all the island creatures, thus making it dangerous and riddled with disease.

The next day Caesar decided to hunt for fish and gather any other edible morsels, in fact anywhere where there appeared to be a glimmer of life. The young heir simply knew that without looking after his health he would not survive. Being totally alone meant he was compelled to be inventive. He needed to make weapons from any materials the island offered up and so he set about scanning every part of his exotic domain. His legacy as the son of a highly skilled hunter and warrior would now present to him the ultimate test. He would need to attune himself to the mind of a primitive hunter-gatherer and, in doing so, provide the nourishment imperative for his basic survival. In fact, in order to build a personal armoury of effective hunting weapons Caesar would require some basic materials from the depths of the island; he would set about this task utilising all his stealth and ingenuity. He proceeded to kick-start his arsenal by constructing a simple hunting knife. He painstakingly foraged in the undergrowth and it didn't take him long to find a large, jagged animal bone which pleased him immensely. After smashing it forcefully with a jagged rock, he chose the largest shard which would be fashioned into the knife's blade. Next, he painstakingly gathered some twisted pieces of rope which had been shed from the cluster of majestic palm trees. He would use these as binding to fashion the handle of his knife. As he surveyed his handiwork, he felt content and proud that he was far more capable than he could ever have imagined. His knife was indeed primitive and imperfect but, without a bow and arrow to firstly kill his prey, he would not be feasting on any flesh anytime soon.

As the dark veil of dusk descended on the island the young prince sat cross-legged on the coarse hessian matting on the floor of his shelter. If he was honest with himself, he knew that his noble father had taught him how to construct hunting weapons and that he should have no issue with making a bow and arrow once he had found suitable materials. He remembered enjoying several hunting expeditions with his father, Saul, in the outback, hunting down antelope, gazelles, bright green lizards and venomous snakes. His father was keen to stress that a bow and arrow was highly effective as it increased the distance between the hunter and his prey and consequently made a kill more likely. Saul had schooled him well and he would now use all his knowledge to practical advantage. He figured that to construct an effective bow he would need a suitably malleable type of wood and so he set about foraging amongst the forest palm trees. Caesar only discovered flimsy sticks and saplings which were easily breakable. Undeterred, he would venture deeper into the forest's undergrowth to find the solution. Soon his patience was rewarded when he stumbled upon a cluster of magnificent English yew trees; *Unusual,* he thought, *for such a tropical climate, so perhaps the Europeans had indeed left their mark.* He fixed his gaze on a sturdy-looking ebony branch, about three hands in length and, upon closer inspection, he realised it bent easily into a 'C' shape that would facilitate the mechanism of a reliable hunting bow. Caesar felt the warm glow of positive optimism radiate through him and his natural ability as a hunter was clearly now in evidence. Any doubts that he had had about his ability to survive began to evaporate like a vapid grey cloud. His next task was to string the bow; this proved quite challenging as he needed the correct length of cord to create suitable tension and tensile strength in the bow to propel the arrows with lightning speed into the ensnared and doomed animals he would select as prey. It was with immense pride that Caesar soon observed his carefully crafted bow and array of arrows. As the day turned to night, he devised a walking map of the area, remembering where he had seen fauna suitable for his hunting needs, the kind of nutritious flesh that would sustain the vital source of protein he needed to keep healthy and strong.

By the next evening the young prince and now extremely capable hunter carried in his homemade hessian sack an impressive catch from the turquoise waters surrounding the island; this included several large rainbow trout, an exotic breed of flat pomfret fish and some curious baby sharks with dusty yellow fins and a few silver-blue eels. Caesar's very successful day's hunting was very pleasing to him and his island catch had indeed exceeded his wildest expectations – the fact that his primitive weapons were so effective gave him some consolation that, although his lonely and solitary life at the present time would be unbearable at times, he could sustain his health and plan his next journey to search for his beloved parents. They were his life-blood and inspiration to stay strong and resilient, and so he kept this perpetual flickering light of optimism constantly in his heart. As he gazed in wonderment at the twinkling stars that night, he thought that their bright constellations were beautiful, scattered like minute diamonds on a velvet blanket of pitch-black. Next, Caesar set about preparing his supper of two garishly red pomfret fish on his primitive fire of banana leaves and twisted pieces of tree bark; when they were devoured and his appetite satiated, he sat back in his encampment and thought about his next plan of action. He had to build a new boat to leave this desolate island he had ventured to and sail away in search of the elusive Vestuku Island. He felt instinctively that his parents had ventured there; this was his resolve to succeed and no matter how arduous the challenges he would conquer them.

Every evening before he slept Caesar like to drink the milk from the lush coconuts that fell frequently from the numerous majestic palm trees scattered around. His machete was made from jagged grey flint: basic and imperfect but extremely useful in splitting open the coconut shell and releasing the bright, white succulent flesh and sweet opaque nectar. He loved to perform this nightly ritual when he could as it invigorated his body and mind and allowed him to sleep soundly, closing his eyes in anticipation of the next day.

As the bright translucent rays of the hot yellow morning enveloped Caesar's encampment, he fetched a piece of decrepit parchment together with his writing tool, a slim chiselled twig tipped in black embers from last night's smouldering fire. He decided to draw a map of his estimated location and, using his limited knowledge of the islands, he tried to deduce where he was now in relation to Vestuku Island – he had clearly sailed off course and needed to head west; his father had taught him about the geography of the islands and had also gifted him a compass as a 16th birthday present. Caesar realised that he had veered northwest and thus landed on a different island. Undeterred, he was determined to build a suitably durable boat and imminently set sail to finally solve the mystery about his parents' whereabouts. It was some 12 months since his parents had left on their mission and he was now a year older and wiser. He worked tirelessly for the next seven days constructing his small wooden boat; he had become quite the competent young builder. It was an arduous task cutting down the palm trees for wood and bringing to life his sturdy vessel which would have to be strong enough to weather the notorious storms which would inevitably confront him.

He worked meticulously like a determined soldier,

checking his handiwork frequently and stopping only to eat supper and refuel his weary body with a few hours of sleep each night. All the blood, sweat and tears were really worth the sacrifice as he managed to construct an impressive wooden boat both sturdy and seaworthy and a rectangular-shaped box which would be invaluable in storing his weapons, fishing rods and supplies of food ready for his voyage. *Not bad for a 17-year-old amateur sailor!*, he thought to himself as he surveyed his new boat with great pride. He was not expecting his quest to find his parents easy and, in fact, there was no guarantee that he *would* even make it, but he felt justified in feeling a real sense of satisfaction and pride in surviving this far. The next morning he would set off to find Vestuku in the arms of Poseidon and a very uncertain future. He took comfort in the hope that Saul and Letitia were still alive; the vision of their beautiful and noble faces was the last thing he saw as his eyes closed for sleep.

Dawn broke over the tropical island that had been Caesar's home for what seemed like an eternity but in fact it had been around 11 months. He awoke from his sleep with a start to the shrill resonating cries from the giant gulls circling around the encampment, indeed a morning ritual that he would be pleased to leave behind. He planned to set sail that evening when the tide was in his favour, and so he busied himself preparing his boat, making an inventory of his equipment, gathering all his belongings and food supplies and checking the boat's main sail. His voyage was imminent and, like an excited child with a new toy, he was keen to see how his boat adapted to the powerful ocean's waves. By the afternoon, way ahead of schedule in fact, the young warrior had organised everything for his voyage; he only had to catch fish for his food supply for the next few days, his fishing rods and nets clutched tightly in his determined hands. He always made a good catch and he felt positive he would secure a tasty array of food for the start of his journey. As he waited for the dancing fish to end their water dance and devour the bait at the end of his fishing rod, he gazed thoughtfully at the striking azure-coloured ocean.

This mysterious, unnamed island where no other inhabitants seemed to exist had indeed proved to be a safe haven, but his loneliness and isolation had frequently been difficult burdens to carry on such young shoulders. With these profound thoughts swirling around his mind, Caesar set about leaving the island. It took all his youthful strength to navigate his boat into the fast-moving waters and, as the waves lashed fiercely, he moved forward with the realisation that his voyage to Vestuku Island would be an extremely arduous and exhausting mission. His limited knowledge of sailing had been acquired by watching his father and Ejuki, the elder, when they took him on fishing trips around their island. Nevertheless, armed with his map and compass he formulated a basic itinerary, a road map to Vestuku and his ultimate goal. It was truly a miracle that he had survived and he was fully aware that his evil uncle would have been so enraged by his escape that he would stop at nothing to find him and murder him. After all, he would go to any lengths to become tribal chief – clearly a man devoid of morals or integrity.

As Caesar awoke to the hot searing rays of the orange sun on his sun-drenched eyes he didn't know how many days he had been drifting in solitude. The constant swaying of the boat must have induced a deep sleep like a baby being rocked in the gentle motions of his cot. He balanced precariously as he searched his supply box for his compass and map of parchment. He estimated that sailing directly north-west for approximately seven days could, in fact, facilitate him in successfully reaching the domain where his parents landed and hopefully where they were still very much alive and well. But right now his extreme hunger and dehydration were uppermost in his mind and consequently he hastily cast his fishing net out into the enveloping foam of the beautiful translucent ocean. His optimism was not in vain; soon he was proudly gazing at his tangled fishing net and the dozen gleaming grey fish as well as the few baby shark entwined in its mesh. He was delighted that his first catch was so abundant and was pleased that, when leaving his island, he had had the foresight to take a large piece of rock salt from Lesotu's house to preserve the food, being fully aware that the theft would have enraged his corrupt nemesis. As he covered his catch in the rough grainy salt he grimaced mischievously – the fish would taste even better knowing that his bold move would have the desired effect. The small, ochre pottery kiln that his mother had left behind was invaluable now; although the breeze was quite strong he managed to make a small flame by rubbing two small twigs together and, once a few fish were gutted and laid out, he managed to half cook them so he had an adequate supper and a tasty supply of protein to last for at least a few days.

The voyage continued at a steady pace; Caesar managed to keep himself adequately nourished and his health did not deteriorate too drastically. The young prince followed his map meticulously and used his trusted compass to guide him and, day by day – which actually still seemed like an eternity – he counted ten sunsets and sunrises before all his efforts were immediately rewarded. On the morning of the eleventh day he saw a miraculous sight. The faint silhouette of a cluster of hazy palm trees ahead indicated that he had finally found an island. He felt a heady excitement and steered his boat with its weather-beaten oars with renewed vigour. Could this finally be

Vestuku Island? Would he finally be reunited with his precious parents? He was soon to uncover the truth and, whatever the revelation, he was proud to have made it this far.

CHAPTER 3

Survival

How elated did he feel at enduring all his hardships and conquering his fears to finally succeed in surviving and moving one step closer to finding out what really transpired when his mother and father failed to return to him?. The young warrior and, in fact now quite accomplished sailor, felt an overwhelming excitement as he truly believed in his heart that he had finally arrived at the island where his parents had ventured. How he missed the warm loving embrace of his mother and the regal mobility and perpetual protection of his father. Would he actually be reunited with them this time? He avoided building up his expectations for them to disintegrate and so he would keep an open mind but remained adamant that he would never give up on finding them. He was steadfast in his mission and unwavering in his resolve. Caesar finally made it onto the island and, as his sunburnt feet hit the golden sand, he felt unsteady and quite lightheaded.

He wondered what would transpire here, his journey had been very challenging and he felt exhausted, his young body weakened and emaciated. He found a nearby cove and concealed his boat which had miraculously delivered him safely. Suddenly he felt faint and nauseous and, fetching his trusty machete, he took advantage of the lush coconuts that had fallen from one of the towering palm trees near the shore. His strength was fading fast but he managed to cut one open. He was fortunate that the translucent coconut water inside was enough to sustain him. A cupful, of this tropical elixir was reviving and a very welcome nourishment in light of his present predicament. Suddenly, Caesar surveyed in the distance the shadowy silhouette of a person moving at pace towards him, and before he even had time to arm himself he was surrounded with at least a dozen ferocious-looking islanders. They circled menacingly like a pack of bloodthirsty hyenas. Caesar had been taken by surprise but to show fear could truly cost him his life. Before he knew it, the tall, imposing figure of the island's chief made his presence felt like a ghostly phantom and Caesar was immediately struck by his disturbing appearance and decidedly evil aura. The strange chief's face was covered in deep, twisted cuts which zigzagged across his decrepit face and his eyes glowed like shards of ebony fire. His manner was confrontational and he wasted no time in addressing this young intruder who had the audacity to trespass.

"I am Chief Fellani and this is Vestuku Island. What is your business here?" he inquired with an inquisitive air of disdain. "What is your name, boy? State your business and be truthful or I'll have no hesitation in feeding your dead carcass to those vicious vultures circling overhead!" Upon realising that he was outnumbered and outgunned, Caesar confessed the real reason that he had made the arduous and extremely perilous journey to Vestuku Island.

"Your Highness, I confess that I have sailed for many weeks from my home on Piku Island in the west in very perilous conditions to find my parents." His voice became increasingly desperate sounding., "My father is the chief and they left over a year ago and their disappearance is a real mystery. So you see my intention is only to find my precious family. I come in peace and sincerely apologise for my unexpected arrival on your magnificent island." Upon hearing this revelation, the chief seemed curiously unnerved and agitated and Caesar immediately felt that he knew the truth about his parents' fate. Caesar remained silent in anticipation of the chief's next move. After a few tense minutes of contemplation the chief declared,

"Yes, you're right, boy; this is indeed Vestuku Island and yes, it seems your parents did visit my dominion, but they departed at least six months ago. I showed them great hospitality and gave them adequate food and supplies to return back to your home, so it's truly a real mystery about their fate!" Again, Caesar was instinctively aware that this was a lie and that, in light of this treachery, he suspected that, sadly, it was most unlikely that Saul and Letitia were still alive and had been callously slaughtered by this cold-hearted tyrant. His first instinct was to flee but he realised it was imperative to keep his nerve and play along with the chief's evil and twisted web of lies. Fellani was no doubt plotting his demise as it wasn't in his interests to allow him to leave and, for now, he explained to Caesar that he was actually welcome to stay in the servants' quarters near his house. He felt compelled to comply as he realised that resistance would inevitably be met with physical restraint. It was regrettable that he felt like a trapped animal, ensnared for now but not without the capability to escape. He would tolerate the situation, so long as he found out the truth about his parents' fate., In his mind he kept the flame of hope alive that his parents were still walking the earth. Only time would tell if his worst nightmare had been played out and his parents were captured or had been slain and buried deep in this hauntingly beautiful tropical island.

As dusk draped its alluring amber cloak over the island, Caesar crept stealthily from the servants' quarters, being very careful not to be followed, and briskly walked the winding path to Fellani's very brightly decorated house. He was very drawn to that location and he felt that it hid many dark secrets. It would be here that he would finally uncover what really transpired when Saul and Letitia first arrived and, subsequently, what their ultimate fate was. Caesar knew that his sudden absence would be noticed by the servants and that the alarm would be raised, so he had to be swift in his actions and perilously covert in all his movements. Fortunately, the back door of Fellani's house was open and he slid in audaciously like a voracious serpent at lightning speed and adept enough to avoid detection. Also, Fellani was not in his residence so the young warrior seized his chance and searched every facet and space for clues as to the whereabouts of his parents. Caesar found nothing and with a very heavy heart went to leave, but as he made for the front door something caught his eye and the stark realisation of what the subject was shook him to his core. It was the turquoise and gold bracelet that his mother always wore and, being so startled by his discovery, he pondered over how Fellani had acquired his mother's possession – either his mother was still alive and on the island or Fellani had murdered her and his father and had very disturbingly kept her jewellery as a macabre memento of his wicked crimes. As he raced back to the servants' quarters in utter shock and disbelief he now felt gravely concerned for the safety of his parents. Nevertheless, he realised it was crucial that he kept his nerve and fight through his mental anguish – with the evil Fellani as his adversary he really had no choice.

The new dawn brought a very unexpected turn of events. Caesar was awoken suddenly by violent knocking and cries from outside the servants' quarters. The village elders informed a startled Caesar that Fellani had been brutally murdered during the night, his throat slit from ear to ear and his house ransacked and stripped of all valuables. He realised that if anyone had seen him around the murder scene the previous night he would undoubtedly have been accused of the bloody deed and immediately executed. He was a young man of great courage and resilience and he resolved to keep his composure and simply plead ignorance about the chief's sudden and untimely demise. As dusk descended on a very traumatic day he felt an urgency to know where his parents had disappeared to and what could possibly have happened to them. He craftily mingled with the group of village elders who had called an emergency meeting to elect Fellani's successor. He had disguised himself well, sitting cross-legged and his head covered with an old shawl like a servant. He was invisible to the elders, appearing insignificant but in fact, in all reality, his mission to solve his parents' disappearance was only just beginning. Fellani's shocking and untimely death had, by a mysterious twist of fate, totally transformed the village dynamic. The murderous tyrant was no more and so Caesar would now be compelled to somehow court favour with one of the elders in order to gain access to their inner circle.

As he sat on the floor, the hard, grim grit of the stone pressing into his flesh, he felt depleted and weary and, although he knew that uncovering the truth of his parents would be extremely difficult, he was blessed with a steely resolve that few possessed. He needed to conjure up this resolve now like a superior magician; he reminded himself that he was a boy capable of feats of bravery and survival that truly belied his tender years. He had been born with a unique power inherited through his bloodline that he could win against all adversity. Now it was crucial that he utilise this gift, and so Caesar was set on his path.

After a while the elders dispersed and, with some trepidation, Caesar waited for the safety of dusk to leave the sacred designated area. Very quickly though, he was confronted and handed over to the head elder who was named Jumani. Caesar was very unnerved by the intensity of his fixed stare and the deep, penetrating tones of his voice. He was well respected on the island and when he asked Caesar what his business was infiltrating their private meeting the young warrior explained about the disappearance of his parents and how he was only seeking answers and, ultimately, closure. Caesar had been taken by surprise and was not at all prepared for Jumani's imminent interrogation;

he vowed to stay strong and keep himself safe. In his heart he wanted to keep the flame of hope burning bright that Saul and Letitia were still alive and safe, but he had an empty feeling of foreboding every time he pictured their faces – could they have already met an untimely demise and become the afterlife? As Jumani led him over the horizon to his house his fate was hanging precariously in the balance – he could only hope to escape the island, with or without his beloved parents. Caesar soon found himself surrounded by Jumani's family and felt very exposed, dangerously outnumbered and outgunned. Indeed, Jumani's wife and three sons instantly fixated on him with icy-cold stares and he was aware that he was in the worst possible spotlight, one in which he wished he could just vanish into thin air. Sadly, no amount of magic could extricate him from this tangled web he now found himself in; he would have to endure but not relent to whatever they had planned for him.

Jumani appeared and immediately beckoned Caesar in who appeared agitated and tense and, most crucially, avoided eye contact with the young prince. Sensing this change in demeanour and attitude, Caesar prepared himself for the worst. He was naturally an optimistic young man but he was under no illusion about how disloyal and ruthless his countrymen could be. He felt that the truth was now imminent so he waited with bated breath for Jumani's revelation.

As predicted, the elderly chief's words were both devastating and final but, in fact, just knowing his parents' fate provided a modicum of resolution and acceptance. After having anticipated this moment for so long, Caesar realised his very future was hanging in the balance. His heart beat quickly as he realised he was just about to find out his parents' fate.

He confessed, "Yes, I must tell you the truth about your parents. They arrived on the island almost two summers ago looking for supplies and arms and stated that they felt threatened by the rumours that the neighbouring villages were plotting to invade. They implored Fellani to take this threat seriously and requested that he should consider forming an alliance to protect their precious villages. As time went on Fellani noticed that they had become very popular with the villages and were highly respected as true African nobility by blood and kinship. In so realising that Saul was of actual royal blood he was. a true threat to his place on the throne. Consequently, he murdered them both as they slept, I'm afraid to say in the most brutal way – mercilessly cutting their throats and discarding the bloody, butchered bodies to the murky depths of the turbulent ocean." Upon hearing Jumani's excruciatingly stark words the young warrior felt truly devastated, his worst fears confirmed. He managed to compose himself but still a stream of salty tears welled up in his tired, vacant eyes as he fought through the searing pain of his distress.

He did in fact have one last question for Jumani and exclaimed, "I really need to know; did you actually witness Jumani killing my parents or were the brutal and barbaric circumstances of their deaths retold to you?" Jumani looked pensive and downcast upon hearing Caesar's request for his honesty and transparency, but he now felt duty-bound to confess all.

"I must admit to you that at first I refused to be part of Fellani's murderous plot but when he threatened the safety of my family I became complicit in his evil deeds. I am not proud of my actions, but all I ask is that you try to understand that I could not risk the safety of *my* loved ones. I was therefore compelled to act as a lookout whilst the fiendish king and his henchman slaughtered your parents in cold blood. From that day to this I have been tortured by guilt and have not slept since. The truth is I'm forever now living in a state of guilt and regret and I'm truly sorry – your parents met such a brutal end, being sent prematurely into the ominously Dark World of Hades." Upon hearing Jumani's confession and having his worst fears confirmed he felt as if his heart and soul had been forcibly ripped from his body. He felt dizzy and disorientated but, fighting through his agony, he mustered the strength to ask Jumani to reveal the location of his parents' remains.

Later, Caesar found himself at a concealed clearing by the edge of the shore, the blanket of sunburnt ochre sand stretched to the edge of a haphazard and uneven mound of rough, coarse earth. This, he realised with much agony, was his parents' final resting place. This gruesome sight made the young warrior feel a searing pain rip through his entire body; he felt unsteady on his feet and suddenly depleted of all strength and fortitude. He caught Jumani's guilty and treacherous stare and realised he had uncovered the horrific truth. He resolved at that moment to lock that particular door; perhaps the future would release it again and give him the closure he so longed for. Only time would tell.

As he reflected on this nightmare scenario and confirmation that his worst fears were reality, he tried to lift his spirits. He contemplated how he could view his parents' painful absence differently. Caesar searched his shattered heart and took comfort in realising that the earthly bodies of Saul and Letitia had simply returned to the earth, but their noble souls, in fact, eternally ageless since their birth, had simply returned to their maker. He placed his foot tentatively on the sunburnt earth of the grave, and as his heart raced he heard the comforting voices of his parents. The dulcet tones were crystal clear and succinct as if they were actually present on the island with him. The younger contemplated this deeply ethereal experience and viewed his precious memories of his parents as a bridge. There was a great sense of love and an everlasting key to open doors into the universe and the magnificent worlds beyond. In this vein, Caesar took some comforting solace in viewing the grave before him as a place to facilitate the exhilaration and positivity of the rebirth of the precious spirits, with the consolation of wishing our deceased loved ones a safe onward journey to the afterlife. He picked up some coarse grains of earth from the grave and let them run through his fingers like the sands of time, bringing force to this special moment. He contemplated to himself, *If I think of the eternal spirits of my beloved mother and father as part of nature now, I will forever remember them as a lush, green forest and I can let them sleep here in beauty for all eternity.* He continued to think profound thoughts about mortality and that the physical being on earth erodes but the eternal spirit exists forever. He contemplated that in this mortal life we can choose to conjure our own devils and succumb to our darkest fears or we can have the ability to create and nurture our own divine angels who guide and protect us and strengthen who we are and, indeed, subsequently who we are destined to become.

Caesar was still deep in thought when Jumani suddenly appeared beside him and warned him that, for his own safety, he must leave the island imminently. He revealed that the other village elders who had been part of Fellani's crime against his parents feared being discovered and so the threat to his life was very real. Jumani spoke about the fact that the elders would often trade goods with passing pirate ships and that one such crew was expected to visit in the next few days. Caesar was instantly intrigued by this and, when he asked about the specific details of such goods, he was told everything from tools, weapons, food and, apparently, men were exchanged for guns; although some may consider this as exploitation, considering his present predicament it seemed quite an attractive prospect and he hoped the start of a new adventure. With that, Caesar was to become part of the pirate crew and Jumani promised him that he would have words with the pirate captain to ensure that he was considered a valuable asset. Astonishingly, Jumani placed four gold coins in his hand. He explained that, despite everything, he was racked with guilt about the way his parents were murdered; although no amount of gold could compensate for his loss he hoped that his gesture could provide a new start for him. Of course, Caesar did not implicitly trust Jumani or anyone else on Vestuku Island. Each day he remained on the island he knew he would be placing his life in grave danger. He resolved to escape with the pirate crew as soon as he could facilitate this.

As the day descended into dusk, Jumani advised Caesar to stay in his home undetected until the pirate crew arrived. He also offered him clothes and food for the journey. He felt nervous about trusting him and realised that, like hunted prey, he could in fact be walking into a deadly trap. Nonetheless, he felt compelled to take his chances with him and his pirate collaborators. As he left the graveside with Jumani he looked up at the heavens and hoped that the spirits of his ancestors would keep him save and guide him. He waited for the band of ruthless cutthroats with whom he would somehow have to survive, but all the while he knew he had the strength of his conviction and sheer determination to succeed no matter what he had to endure.

CHAPTER 4

Pirate Life

As the first bright lights of dawn dripped its translucent glow over the island, the year was 1693 and the Golden Age of Piracy was in full decadent flow, from the tropical waters of the Caribbean, the North American coast, the precious West African waters to the magnificent Indian Ocean. Caesar would have never envisaged himself sailing the high seas with a band of ruthless, cutthroat renegades, the unfortunates whom society had persecuted and discarded, those vulnerable souls who were not deemed worthy of mercy or respect – in fact, an invisible underclass whose lives were deemed expendable and worthless.

Young Caesar, that unique and incredibly resilient warrior, was eager to be indoctrinated into the dubious and menacingly murky world of piracy. He didn't have the privilege of morality or stability and, now finding himself completely alone and isolated, he would simply take his chances with the sons of the notorious black flag. He had heard stories of former black slaves being granted their freedom as well as gold, land and titles in exchange for a devoted and loyal service aboard the pirate crews. This situation was by no means befitting for a prince of royal blood, but it would serve its purpose as a means to escape this evil island and the deeply decadent and unpredictable clutches of the elders and their future leader. He believed it was far–better to immerse himself in a world where danger and immorality were expected ways of life rather than remain in the poisonous company of the island's conspirators who were adept at lulling an individual into a false sense of security only to betray and murder – on command without conscience or mercy – as his parents had learned to their detriment, paying the ultimate price with their precious lives.

After two sunsets had arisen, Jumani informed Caesar that the pirate ship had been sighted by his son and so Caesar was hastily instructed to gather together his small bag of belongings and to wait by the shore in this carefully concealed stone cave, the inventive hideout that only Jumani's family knew about. Once Caesar had transferred his meagre belongings to the raw stone abode he stood excitedly by the shoreline; his tired eyes were blurry, but he could just make out the faint silhouette of a ship. Caesar thought its progress to be deceptive. From his vantage point the pirate entourage seemed light years away in the distance but, in reality, this particular crew were speeding along at pace. Perhaps this was due to the fact that its captain was none other than captain Henry Avery, a very accomplished and successful buccaneer, a formidable adversary and ruthless master of the high seas.

Caesar spotted a glimpse of a garish red flag attached to the top of the pirate ship's mast; it billowed in the cool African breeze and was very different from the usual black and white Jolly Roger pirate flag. In fact, this was a very distinctive and unique feature for this particular English captain, Henry Avery, otherwise known as Long Ben or Captain Bridgeman. Apparently, when the red flag was hoisted it was a gruesome reminder that, once captured on his ship, Avery decreed that no man would ever be spared.

So now it was just a curious waiting game for Caesar; he was compelled to involve himself in whatever dubious business Jumani and Avery were complicit in. He knew his imminent voyage would be incredibly difficult and that he would be compelled against his better judgement to carry out barbaric and criminal acts that would not sit easily with him in light of his moral and righteous upbringing. He thought to himself that he could endure it if he viewed his pirate identity an enforced role he was playing, but he vowed never to poison his soul in the pursuit of money and prestige. He was determined that his new pirate life would not destroy his virtuous and noble nature as an

Ashanti heir. He knew deep down this new path would have many challenges and pitfalls and his survival was therefore crucial: priority one was to eventually return to his village to claim his crown and take his rightful place as King. This was imperative to secure his bloodline and the survival of his people. So for now he would embrace his pirate life; he prayed it would not be long before he could once again enjoy the warmth and nurturing embrace of his distant homeland.

Under the covert cloak of dusk Captain Avery's magnificent pirate ship *The Charles II*, otherwise known as *The Fancy*, finally arrived on Vestuku Island that very night. Jumani appeared at the cave hideout and excitedly informed and intrigued a decidedly cautious Caesar about the bold and decadent world of Captain Avery and how he had such a close business relationship with him. He was fully aware that Jumani's business dealings with Avery were very much illegal and that of course he would embellish and manipulate the truth for his own financial gain. Jumani made it crystal clear to Caesar that he would have to agree to Avery's demands in order to facilitate him being allowed to become a crewmember on his ship and that his word was law and not open to negotiation. Caesar suspected that the actual truth of their long history of transactions involving villagers of low rank were both inhumane and deeply immoral. It transpired the pirate Captain such as Avery regarded black slaves as lucrative and enduring cargo; they were utilised as labour on the ships, but more significantly they were eventually transported to the Americas as quickly and cheaply as possible.

These unfortunate Africans would consequently be sold to labour in treacherous conditions on coffee, tobacco, cocoa, and sugar and cotton plantations. They were also found in gold and silver mines, rice fields, the construction industry, carpenters to cut timber for ships as skilled labour and, heartbreakingly, as lowly domestic servants. It was apparent that some chosen black crewmembers were granted their freedom, but this was dependent on the decision and intention of that particular pirate ship and whether their captain was humane. Caesar listened to Jumani's revelations with curiosity tinged with deep distrust. Apparently, Avery had initially been part of the Royal Navy and then worked as a privateer on military ships commandeered by governments and sovereign states. One such expedition was on a 46-gun military ship called *The Charles II*, which was a Spanish service ship in the employ of the King of Spain. The crew was mostly English who were incensed with the conditions they had to endure and the inhumane treatment they received. Avery therefore decided with the crew to declare mutiny, and so in 1694 the ship became *The Fancy* and the men began their amazing descent into piracy that included attacking English and

Dutch merchants off the coast of Africa. Caesar was struck by how impressed Jumani seemed by Avery's criminal activity and he announced that the Captain had arrived and he would greet him immediately. He explained to Caesar that he should prepare himself to leave the island in a few days' time and that he would arrange everything for him with Avery so that all parties would be satisfied with him joining the crew. A few days passed and the young warrior wondered what had transpired between Jumani and Avery and his duplicitous and dubious pirate crew. These were men who would not flinch at bloody murder if they believed there was financial gain to be had; they were after all truly the most callous and cold-hearted souls. Caesar thought that perhaps, as youngsters, they had been moral and pure but now the years of vicious barbaric murder and theft had blackened their hearts beyond recognition and that there was never any hope of redemption for them. He decided to defy Jumani's instruction and wait in the cave; he felt compelled to uncover the real truth about Avery's involvement with the islanders. He had a dark feeling of foreboding and knew instinctively that he may not like what he was about to uncover. As soon as the chief elder's house was in sight and there was no imminent prospect of being discovered, Caesar positioned himself audaciously right outside, adjacent to the parlour, in the hope of listening to his conversation with Avery.

It wasn't long before Jumani could be heard laughing and peering through the hessian curtain covering the front door of the hut. Caesar spied, in all his decadent glory, a dark, swarthy and indeed menacing figure dressed in flamboyant crimson velvet and fine calico. His weather-beaten face looked like he had endured a thousand battles and his deep scars were testament to a gruesome and barbaric career on the high seas. Captain Avery indeed looked even more formidable and treacherous a man than Caesar could ever have imagined.

As he listened intently to their muffled words he caught Avery uttering, "We will leave tomorrow evening and I have agreed to trade my precious cargo for five of your men; they will work as crew and I expect them to be loyal and devoted. These words had a haunting finality about them and he was of course one of the new recruits, hired on labour for the cunning Avery. He obviously saw the men as disposable goods and the callous Jumani was a willing and duplicitous accomplice.

Caesar made his way back to the shore feeling powerless in his present predicament. Avery was clearly a deeply immoral man who had prospered from the illegal trade with unfortunate and desperate slaves. He felt entitled in treating human beings as merely replaceable goods. He was still contemplating this when he heard hurried footsteps approaching the stone cavern that had been his home for the last two weeks. The distinct silhouette of Jumani could be seen and he beckoned Caesar to gather his sparse belongings and join Avery's crew.

"Come now, boy! There is no time to wait! Captain Avery is waiting for you to set sail. Bring your possessions and follow me. Look lively!"

Caesar grabbed his small yellow jute bag and threw in his few worldly possessions: the compass his father had gifted him, a shiny silver dagger (which one of the elders had given him for protection), a collection of faded and threadbare clothes, a few trinkets from his mother and – most precious of all – his late father's jade and gold dragon signet ring. He swiftly ran like a lithe gazelle to Avery's ship; resistance was now futile, only initiative and ingenuity would save him now. With steely determination resonating in his young mind he boarded *The Charles II*. He looked upwards at the garish red and white pirate flag, hoisted high on its white pole, its faded, decrepit fabric billowing in the cool dusk air. As he looked back at the island which he now knew for certain was sadly the burial ground of his beloved parents, he felt both melancholic and unsettled, but was about to embark on the next chapter of his young life. He was now entering uncharted territory amongst the new pirate crew and, although he was anticipating very challenging situations and difficult conditions, he would just make the most of this experience that would inevitably shape his future. He watched the shoreline disappear and was deep in his own thoughts when he suddenly felt a rough hand forcefully striking his shoulder.

As he turned around he saw a swarthy-looking dark-haired pirate who exclaimed, "I'm your Captain, Thomas Avery. I've been looking forward to meeting you. Jumani tells me you are of tribal royal blood and that's very interesting, but do you have what it takes to make the grade as a ruthless pirate?" Caesar was stunned into silence but managed to utter a few audible words.

"I am very pleased to meet you, Captain, and I will not let you down. I am brave beyond my years and I am determined to prove myself to you!"

Avery grimaced, his bright blue eyes gleaming mischievously, who simply responded, "That's good, a pirate's life for you now! Go to the ship's hulk and settle in. We will speak again in the morning and I will instruct you on your duties on my ship. I paid handsomely for you. Jumani, I hope, has guided me well!"

The next morning Caesar was summoned to Avery's quarters by Levington, the senior galley-master, a brutish man devoid of manners or any semblance of decorum. He made it clear that he didn't approve of the fact that Avery apparently favoured him and warned him not to get above his station. Caesar thought it wise not to respond to the hostile threats; instead he simply smiled but making sure to look him straight in the eye to send a message to this despicable villain that he was not scared. They were like two wild animals confronting each other before an inevitable fight, but Levington he would deal with later. Avery beckoned him on and so he stayed focused on impressing the captain and securing his place with the crew.

Avery opened the door of his quarters with lightning speed, not even giving Caesar time to knock. He seemed a very determined and forthright character and his appearance and physicality were strikingly memorable. He insisted his newly acquired crewmember perch on one of the luxurious and embroidered armchairs that adorned his domain.

Avery was well into his middle ages, his mop of raven black hair flecked with woven silver threads, his head tilted to one side curiously and his tall, lithe physique coiled around his chair like a predatory serpent. His face was heavily lined and there was a deep jagged scar running from his right eye all the way down to his jaw. His eyes quite unnerved Caesar; they looked like pools of azure fire and were in fact quite hypnotic.

He simply stared at his new crewmember with a terrifying fixed gaze. He remained silent at first and then, after a few minutes, uttered these truly menacing words, "I understand from what Jumani told me that you are the son and heir to the Ashanti tribe on Piku Island and my informants tell me that your uncle is now crowned King in your absence. Your parents were murdered on Vestuku Island and you have now been sold to me for 20 gold sovereigns. That is your position now and so if you prove to be a loyal and hard-working member of my crew I may decide to grant you your freedom. I have done so on occasion with black slaves on the plantations who became my property. I'm sure you must realise that on my ship your noble birth is irrelevant. I've been told you are literate and can use a compass and maps and so you will have the honour of assisting me directly. All crew receive wages according to how useful they are to me and you will be my eyes and ears. You will observe and report daily to me about the crew's conduct and inform me of any treachery or plot against me by the men. And so you see it really is to your advantage to serve me well. We will see in time exactly what kind of man you are and if you have the courage and strength to survive the pirate life."

CHAPTER 5

The Legend of a Pirate

The year was 1700 and Caesar had become a very successful and skilled captain aboard *The Aquila*. It was an amazement to himself that the last four years had been, on one hand, perilous and murderous and his soul was now deeply drenched in the crimson blood of his adversaries. On the other he had prospered financially beyond his wildest expectations. Although the source of this affluence was suspect and definitely not a badge of honour, in time he would use it to secure the future of his village and take his rightful place on the throne as King....

Caesar had amassed a fortune by firstly attacking mainly Spanish ships around the coast of the Bahamas and Cuba and had been particularly successful along the southeastern Florida coast. A place called Elliott Key had served as his home and had consequently proved to be immensely lucrative. The plundering of small villages and decimating lone vessels became a way of life; he was merciless in his pursuit of wealth and the prestige and notoriety that afforded this decadent lifestyle. His mentor and confidant, the notorious Captain Thomas Avery, had apparently absconded to the dark depths of England and after so long Caesar frequently wondered what fate had bestowed on him. The rumour mill swirled in favour of him now being in London and Caesar had an inclination to perhaps visit the capital city to meet him. He had a deep curiosity about Avery. Maybe if Neptune's tides were favourable this would soon be satisfied.

Meanwhile, in the deep, dark depths of Avery's likely lair – namely the City of London – a young lad who would prove to be a loyal and uniquely trustworthy crewmember was having a turbulent time. His name was Jack Gibson, a fast and resourceful boy of some 16 years.

So indeed, who was this mysterious youth? A poor unfortunate destined for a life of hardship or perhaps the son of a nobleman who had unfortunately fallen on hard times?

The boy was such a handsome young fellow with his piercing blue eyes and shock of ebony black hair...

The stark truth was, in fact, that he was a London orphan whose parents and sister had perished from the fever; having been cast out onto the murky and menacing streets of London he survived by becoming a skilled pickpocket and fencer. He had battled through many hardships and eventually found lodgings with a fellow thief and unfortunate named Sam until, one evening, he returned to their digs and found his friend savagely slaughtered and his blood spilled in a truly gruesome fashion. In fact, his head had been decapitated and his hands cut off. Jack thought that this was alarmingly ritualistic and he wondered what Sam had done to warrant such a brutal and premature end to his life. Jack had no tine to extricate himself from this nightmare scenario as he was swiftly arrested, told that he was suspected of murder and led away by two burly police officers. He glanced back at the squalid tenement that had been his home for months; his future was now really bleak and he thought that without the faint glimmer of hope he could now be plunged into a pit of total despair.

He found himself in a squalid prison cell where his wrists were chained above his head and the only chink of light could be seen through the bars of a small window opposite where he laid down. He was thirsty and emaciated and had even lost count of the days he had been incarcerated in this pit of hell.

Jack also suffered savage whippings from the sadistic jailer, Lynch, and, although he declared his innocence throughout this torture, his protestations fell on deaf ears.

One morning in a very unexpected turn of events, he was taken by prison transport to the docks and told that he was being transported to a remote jail on an island. Without being granted a trial and the opportunity to prove his innocence the young lad felt very despondent and isolated.

As he sat in his squalid cell on a blanket of straw, like an ensnared animal in a cage, Jack felt so depleted and apprehensive. Realising that this excruciating feeling of loneliness and despair could be his undoing he slipped a blanket around himself and pulled it tight, just waiting for death to claim his soul and end his unbearable torment.

After what seemed an eternity, but was in fact only a few weeks, Jack was startled one evening by the metallic clatter of the prison guard's keys and, to his amazement, in shuffled a very dishevelled, grey-haired and wizened old man who was unsteady on his feet and frail. At first he would not utter a word to Jack and just crouched in the corner like a wounded animal, but eventually he spoke in an unusual Italian dialect and introduced himself as Salvatore. He relayed to a curious Jack that he had previously been a priest in Rome but that, due to his prolific addictions to alcohol and gambling, had been excluded from the Church permanently and accused of stealing money. He had already served ten years in this despicable jail.

It was difficult for Jack to guess the exact age of this frail and decrepit son of God but he noticed the blue of his eyes still shone bright in stark contrast to his heavily lined and ravaged features; his long silver beard aged him mercilessly. Jack listened intently as Salvatore revealed that his life had been destroyed 20 years previously when he stabbed an innkeeper to death in a frenzied attack and had been convicted to life on this island fortress. Jack made sure always to share his meagre rations of putrid soup and mouldy bread with his desperately ill cell-mate.

After a few weeks Salvatore informed Jack that he felt close to death and that he wanted to leave him his legacy; he had no son and heir and believed that his gift would change Jack's life forever.

As the morning released a faint glow through the barred window directly above his sleeping area in the squalid cell, Jack noticed that Salvatore had been unusually active and he handed him an old piece of very faded parchment. The old priest instructed a startled Jack to memorise the contents in detail and destroy it by whatever means at his disposal. He also gifted to a very startled Jack a beautifully ornate silver dagger and advised him to only use the unique weapon when he was certain his life was in mortal danger. Salvatore had really taken Jack by surprise but in the most positive of circumstances. The old priest explained that, before he was defrocked and banished from the Church, he had found the mysterious map hidden in the back of a Bible, which miraculously the evil head jailer, Lynch, had permitted him to keep.

Upon scrutinising the paper-thin parchment, Jack could just about make out the faded letters – Santorini – and so, although the map was barely legible, at least he knew the elusive treasure was located off the coast of Italy. It was not in Jack's nature to be naturally tactile but he was so overwhelmed by sheer exhilaration and excitement that he hugged Salvatore, an embrace that would fit well as if they were father and son. Salvatore grinned as Jack enthusiastically promised that upon his imminent escape he would uncover the treasure and fulfil his legacy. Having carefully and meticulously memorised every detail of the Santorini treasure map, Jack handed the parchment to the old priest who used the last candle remnants to burn the evidence into a smoky pile of smouldering ashes.

Sadly, in the days that followed Salvatore's visit, his frail health deteriorated very rapidly and Jack felt scared and distraught. He had become accustomed to the old priest's sparkling intellect and dry sense of humour; in fact he knew that, without this unique support camaraderie, he may have deteriorated mentally and perished in the pit of despair that his life's circumstances had placed him in. As the prison chaplain was hastily ushered in to read Salvatore his last rites, Jack flinched, he felt the haunting presence of The Grim Reaper, his shiny silver scythe glinting in the dark depths of Hades, ready to claim the priest who had fallen from grace and whose fate it was to travel over the river to meet his spiritual fate. His time had run out and, as his eyes closed for the last time, Jack felt overwhelmed by grief and, as the hot salty tears cascaded down his face, he managed to compose himself and promised himself that he would escape this unbearable bondage, honour his old friend by claiming the precious treasure and fulfil the Legacy so graciously bestowed on him.

The guards were immediately summoned to prepare the late Salvatore's body for burial at sea the next morning and it was a grief-stricken Jack who watched intensely as they wrapped the dead body in coarse hessian cloth, binding it from head to toe like an Egyptian pharaoh preparing for his descent into the underworld. The young treasure hunter felt cheated that Salvatore had left him after enjoying only six months of friendship, but at the same time he was grateful for this fallen priest who, in his eyes, had redeemed himself beyond recognition as his personal friend, teacher, confidant and mentor. As Jack reflected he suddenly had a flash of inspiration that could facilitate an imminent escape from this hellish island jail. In fact, it was well known that the Chateau San Sebastien Jail was notorious for being an impenetrable fortress – no inmate had ever been successful in escaping.

Jack realised that if he switched his body with Salvatore's he would be cast into the unforgiving ocean that was extremely perilous, could result in him drowning and never escaping the cruel clutches of his incarceration. He decided this was a risk worth taking and he felt the spiritual presence of the old priest; he was aware that he now had a guardian angel that was a perpetual presence and instilled in him a fortitude that was both unique and deeply ethereal.

It wasn't an easy task in the early hours of the morning to remove Salvatore's lifeless corpse from his shroud and position him against the cell wall, but he endured and he covered him in the ragged blue blanket that he slept in each arduous night, paying particular attention to covering his head to give the impression that it was him sleeping deeply and not his deceased old friend. Jack then positioned himself inside the hessian bag on the freezing damp stones of the cell floor and, starting from his feet, he laced up both sides of the death shroud, and when he reached his head he made sure to create two small holes adjacent to his nose and mouth to enable him to breathe. This escape plan was of course very perilous and there was a very good chance that Jack would be caught in his deception, but he knew that unless he seized this golden opportunity to flee he would never escape his unbearable incarceration. As he waited in his hessian shroud – rather like an ensnared animal would – Jack contemplated his precarious situation. He was risking his life with his devious deception as failure and exposure would only lead to the guillotine and his immediate execution.

Jack woke up with a start as he felt the guards lift his rigid body up; his heart beat so fast he felt as if he would pass out... he just had to keep his composure and his nerve. He could smell faintly the delicious scent of freedom. He now just needed to succeed in his escape and be overpowered by its victorious aroma. The prison guards were a pair of rough brutes and under the full control of the evil jailer, Lynch. It wasn't long before Jack felt their dark and deadly presence and, much to his horror, he heard him instruct his staff to bind the body with sturdy chains to ensure it didn't float to the surface of the azure ocean. Jack heard his despicable captor laughing and making insulting remarks about Salvatore and he was seething with rage at the cruel disrespect and inhumane cruelty. The chains were coiled around Jack's body like a devouring metal snake and he suddenly felt extremely constrained and claustrophobic. Jack had not anticipated this cruel twist of fate of course and acknowledged that his only glimmer of hope was to grab the keys from around Lynch's key chain that was hooked to the side of his belt in a typically provocative and menacing way to remind the prisoners that escape was a futile pursuit. Jack loosened the leather ties on the bag and, when he felt himself being lifted up to be thrown into the ocean, he caught a glimpse of the monstrous Lynch. As he was propelled over the edge of the wall he managed to grab Lynch's belt keys and drag him into the deep blue sea with him. A vicious struggle ensued and Jack resisted Lynch who thrashed about defiantly like a wild shark. The battle was only over when the wicked jailer's lifeless body drifted off and Jack frantically managed to unlock himself and emerge victorious, swimming away on the surface of the ocean, its steady, rippling waves carrying him along. Jack was just so relieved that his very precarious plan had been a success and that he now had a fighting chance of survival in finding Salvatore's mysterious hoard of treasure. His eyes, bleary and drenched in ocean salt, just about made out the faint image of a distant island and, although he was exhausted and emaciated, he swam towards it until he became entangled in a twisted mesh of seaweed, passing out in the searing heat.

Jack was unaware of how and when he woke up on the island but he just recalled opening his eyes and realising that the seaweed had enveloped his frail torso and had somehow deposited him on the hot yellow sand. He was startled into consciousness as he soon heard muffled voices around him that became more audible and menacing as they approached. Suddenly, he felt excruciating pain in his back as he was kicked and then was horrified by the rough bejewelled hand that was now wrapped around his throat like a vicious viper. Jack noticed a forbidding shadow looming over him and was soon to be introduced to Henri Caesar, the notorious black pirate whose reputation indeed preceded him.

As Henri Caesar loosened his vice-like grip on Jack's bruised and raw throat he threw him with such force on to the sand it made the boy writhe in agony.

"What is your name, boy?" Caesar bellowed in his broad African accent.

Tentatively, Jack uttered, "It's Jack, Sir, and my family name is Gibson. I am English and I come in peace; I mean no harm."

"OK, boy, but how did you arrive alone here? Where is the rest of your crew? I think you have a lot to hide and you know I don't tolerate betrayal and lies!"

He ordered his foreman, Meadows, to guard Jack and, as he glared at the startled prisoner with his cold, jet-black eyes, there now seemed no way out of this devilish web he found himself tangled up in.

That evening as dusk descended and several vibrant amber bonfires were lit, the captain returned, and with a wry and sarcastic sneer on his weather-beaten face, he gathered his shady crew of renegades and regally declared, "Now, boy, if you want to join my precious crew on my ship, *The Aquila*, you must win your place by fighting my best man... I have the perfect opponent for you... and you must defeat him to gain your place! Mackenzie is the best skilled fighter on

my ship, so if you value your life you'd better shine!"
Caesar uttered this with a cruelly callous grin on his
face, in fact, just like a man devoid of any mercy, intent
on compelling Jack to suffer the cruellest and most
brutal of fates. Jack noticed that a fighting area had
been prepared on the beach and the crew congregated
excitedly like a pack of hungry hyenas waiting for
nourishment – in this case, the most barbaric of blood
sports – two opponents fighting to the death with
no escape clause or reprieve. Jack is ushered to the
makeshift arena and immediately recoils in horror at
the sight of the much-feared fighter, Mackenzie. He
is truly a raw brute of a man, towering well over six
feet tall and covered in a colourful array of tattoos.
Jack could feel his evil gaze focus on his face so he
made a strategic effort to avert this by fixating on
Mackenzie's rough, scarred hands which looked lethal
enough to kill a man with a single savage blow. Jack
instinctively knew that he was not physically capable
of overpowering this beast of a man, so his only hope
of victory was to utilise the silver dagger that Salvatore
had gifted him (miraculously still concealed around
the ankle of his weatherworn leather boots, having
remained unclaimed by the ocean), which at this
pivotal moment in his life was indeed a fortuitous twist
of fate. Caesar was in fact seated on a throne-like chair
to survey the barbaric fight and Jack glanced at him
furtively. The ruthless Captain sneered mercilessly like

a bloodthirsty wolf relishing the ensuing bloodshed and unstripped carnage. The young boy realised that only a miracle could save him now.

"You wretched little maggot, I'm going to enjoy killing you!" Mackenzie snarls as Jack steps into the arena, his heart racing at lightning speed, managing to compose himself and survey his formidable opponent. The bloodthirsty crew cheer as the big brute attacks Jack with a big right overhand punch, Jack swiftly stepping out of range; but before he can bring his hands up to defend himself, Mackenzie drives his shoulder with such force into Jack's chest that he sinks to his knees in agony but manages to clamber to his feet in a deeply dazed and confused state. Mackenzie takes full advantage and lands several solid punches into Jack's gut who is winded and staggers away in a vain attempt to maintain his composure. With his last show of strength, Jack rapidly reaches into his boot and, with the small dagger clutched in his faltering fingers, runs towards an unguarded Mackenzie, plunging the sharp silver blade into his foot and leaving Captain Henri Caesar and the crew aghast at the scene now unfolding. The brute tumbled like a cumbersome giant onto the hot golden sand and Jack swiftly seized his opportunity to pull the blood-drenched dagger out and plunge it up to the hilt into Mackenzie's exposed chest. Jack stands in stunned silence as he realises the enormity of his victory and Henri Caesar and his crew start clapping and cheering like a thirsty Roman crowd celebrating the achievement of one of their illustrious and precious gladiators.

The animated Captain beckons over an overwhelmed-looking Jack and exclaims, "I'm amazed at you, boy, you are quite an accomplished fighter for a boy so pale and thin. You deserve a few jars of rum for our unique entertainment this day. Go get on board my ship, it's called *The Aquila*; the men will show you the way. Tomorrow I will reveal to you my precious Pirate Code. Learn it well, boy... learn it well!"

The next morning Jack found himself aboard *The Aquila*. He was a sensible and resourceful lad; he sold his keg of rum to the men in exchange for food and clothing and he even managed to acquire an antique cross on a chain... he figured that this was a wise move considering how often on board this decadent vessel he would feel compelled to repent for his sins. His late parents had raised him as a God-fearing young man and he hoped not to be too corrupted by his present predicament.

He clambered up on deck with a positive air of renewed optimism and the rest of the crew looked over suspiciously with deep disdain. Suspicious of his position within the crew and absorbed by the green eye of envy, Jack clearly needed to watch his back at all times...

The formidable sight of Henri Caesar, a tall man of stocky build standing well over six feet tall, immediately confronted Jack. His ebony face was deeply creased with age and bore numerous battle scars, the most prominent running from his ear and extending to his jaw. His head was shaven and his ears were adorned with gold earrings and a curious ruby-encrusted medallion hung around his neck. He added to his already menacing appearance by brazenly wearing two gilded silver swords on either side of his waist. A bandoleer stuffed with numerous pistols and knives were strapped horizontally across his chest ready for any imminent danger.

His life of piracy had indeed made him wealthy and his fine clothes, jewellery and other decadent assets were testament to this. He wore a heavy black velvet coat adorned with gleaming gold buttons and his flamboyant long black boots were made from the finest Spanish leather.

Other pirates feared him and his reputation definitely preceded him... He could facilitate his crewmembers becoming wealthier than their wildest dreams but this of course had a forfeit to pay, and of course he demanded his crew's ultimate loyalty and devotion. *The Aquila* was a magnificent ship and the dark temptation of mutiny was a perpetual threat. Consequently, Caesar was adamant that any hint of rebellion or betrayal was immediately extinguished and punished by execution without any reprieve or mercy. Jack was startled when, in full view of the entire crew, Caesar turns to him and stares directly at him, his terrifying ebony eyes a glaring assault on his senses – but he dare not avert his gaze for fear of reprisals. Caesar orders Jack to go below deck to fetch a bucket of water and a brush to scrub the deck and, with a twisted sneer, declares he will be back to inspect every inch of it.

Jack works industriously and makes a point of keeping his head down for the duration to avoid the menacing looks from the deeply envious and hostile crew.

As dusk descends on *The Aquila* the Captain appears and at first stands over Jack in a strange, cold silence.

"Can you read and write, boy? Get to your feet and answer me!" he snarls impatiently.

Jack swiftly clambers to his feet and tries to reply in a respectful tone.

"Oh yes, Captain, I am fortunate that my parents taught me to both read and write."

Caesar places a curious scroll of yellow parchment tied neatly with black silk ribbon on the ledge leading to the galley stairs below. "Read and memorise the contents well, boy, as in the morning I will test you... I expect no error to be made, so make haste, boy. Retire to your quarters... that's an order!"

As Jack descended the stairs to the ship's hulk and the grim threadbare hammock, which would be his bed, he carefully unfolded the scroll and there on the faded pages were all the details of Caesar's Pirate Code. It seemed the detail would be a challenge to learn but Jack was determined to impress as for now it appeared that the ruthless Captain Caesar and *The Aquila* were his only hope of survival.

That evening, reclined in his hammock in a dingy corner of the overcrowded and hedonistic hulk, Jack managed to use the remnants of an old candle to illuminate his area enough for him to read the old pieces of faded parchment. Jack realised that even scallywags had to adhere to a set of rules and he started reading the Captain's Pirate Code with a real sense of wonderment and intrigue:

"**11 Rules of my Pirate Code:**

1.   Implement 'Rock the Vote'

I decree that every man shall have an equal vote in the affairs of the moment. He shall have an equal title to the fresh provisions or strong liquors at anytime seized and shall use them at pleasure unless a scarcity makes it necessary for the common good that a reduction of use or a restriction may be voted on and implemented.

2. Be Wise / Smart: Don't Steal From Pirates

Every man shall be called fairly in turn by the list on board of prizes, because over and above their proper share, they are allowed a shift of clothes. If they dare to defraud the company in fact to the value of one dollar in plate, jewels or money, being marooned will be their punishment. If any man robs another he shall have his nose and ears slit and be put ashore where he shall be sure to encounter extreme hardships.

3. Gambling for Landlubbers

On my ship no crew shall game for money, either with dice or cards.

4. Mind the Curfew

The lights and candles shall be extinguished at eight at night, and if the crew desire to drink after that hour they shall sit upon the open deck without lights.

5. Keep Battle-ready

Each crew shall keep his piece, cutlass and pistols ready at all times, clean and ready for action.

6. Never Bring Your Date Home

No small boy or woman shall be allowed amongst them. If any man shall be found seducing one of the latter sex and carrying her to sea in disguise he shall suffer death.

7. Stand by Your Hearties

He that shall desert the ship or his quarters in the time of battle shall be punished by death or marooning.

8. Settle Disputes Onshore (with pistols and cutlasses of course)

None shall strike another on board the ship, but everyman's quarrel shall be ended onshore by sword or pistol in this manner: at the word of command from the Quartermaster, each man being previously placed back to back, shall turn and fire immediately. If any man does not, the Quartermaster shall knock the piece out of his hand. If both miss their aim they shall take to their cutlasses and he that draws first blood shall be declared the victor.

9. Lose a Limb, Get Workers' Compensation

Every man who succumbs to injury, becomes a cripple or loses a limb in the service shall have eight hundred pieces of eight from the common stock, and for lesser hurts proportionately.

10. Remember Rank has its Privileges

The Captain and the Quartermaster shall each receive two shares of a prize: the Master Gunner and Boatswain, one and a half shares, and all other officers one and one quarter, and private gentlemen of fortune can expect one share each.

11.   Make Sure to Give the Band a Break

On the ship all musicians shall have a rest day on the Sabbath Day (Sunday) only, by right. On all other days by favour only, at the Captain's discretion.'

The next morning Jack awoke in the squalid hulk of *The Aquila* wrapped in his dirty and threadbare hammock. The disturbing sight of scurrying mice was an assault to his eyes but he reconciled that, realistically, this would become part of his morning ritual.

As his feet hit the cold wood of the hulk's floor he felt a sharp and sudden blow to the back of his head and, as he turned around, his gaze fixed upon the ship's foreman, Meadows, an evil and hard-faced convicted murderer whose brutality and ruthlessness was well-documented amongst the crew. He was an English cutthroat and his appearance conveyed that of a ramshackle beggar or a deeply disturbed drunk. It was apparent to Jack that the crew were terrified of him and that he should be very strategic and careful in how he navigated his way around such a devilish brute. He was of middle age with a muscular physique and his hair about his shoulders comprised of thick, matted black dreadlocks. His haggard face showed little emotion and his eyes were as cold as the ocean. He was perpetually surveying his territory and he really didn't miss a trick. As soon as Jack felt Meadows' hateful blow he realised that the jealous hatred the men had for him would only deepen and that Meadows was the chief architect of the smear campaign against him. He could no longer ignore his unnerving sense of impending doom. The Santorini treasure was the only glimmer of hope for him in his very difficult and lonely life and he resolved to stay vigilant and focused no matter what conflicts he had to endure.

Meadows glared at Jack and ordered him to the kitchen to fetch and serve Caesar's breakfast. He reappears with an ornate silver tray laden with a sumptuous feast worthy of the King himself. Placed upon it were a silver coffee pot, fine bone china teacups, saucers and serving plates laden with the finest bread, fruit, meats and spices; indeed, very grand for the Prince of Thieves. Jack laughed to himself at the deep irony of that morning's events.

He knocked tentatively on the door of the Captain's quarters and Caesar boomed in his deep African accent, "Enter, boy; I'm famished, look lively!"

Jack was immediately struck by how very luxurious and grand the Captain's rooms were and he contemplated that, so far in his devilish life, things had been very lucrative indeed... Jack found himself in the Captain's quarters consisting of a bedroom with an adjoining study and at the rear a bathroom area and sitting room with a large closet to house the Captain's elegant and flamboyant clothes...

Captain Henri Caesar was clearly now accustomed to the finer things in life and Jack was in awe at all he surveyed. An elegantly carved oak four-poster bed draped in rich crimson velvet blankets adorned with intricate gold thread, the finest French muslin sheets and elegant silver candlesticks were in stark contrast to the extreme squalor and decay of the rest of *The Aquila*'s facilities.

Jack carefully placed the Captain's breakfast at his place in the dining area and, as he made his way back, he glimpsed Caesar sitting at his desk looking through his numerous maps, charts and compasses. He looked very preoccupied and professional but Jack could not ignore the trail of dried blood encircled around Caesar's antique, ornate and throne-like chair, perhaps the aftermath of a futile attempt at mutiny or the aftermath of Caesar's legendary temper.

Either way, Jack was still contemplating his gruesome vision when Caesar suddenly snaps, "So, boy, let's see how well you know my Pirate Code... now recite point 8 and just be mindful I don't accept mistakes or incomplete or sloppy answers.!"

Jack felt the Captain's icy stare penetrate his bones and his heart raced faster out of sheer apprehension."

That's 'Settle Disputes Ashore', Sir," Jack stammers, but despite his initial nerves he manages to quote this part of the code perfectly word for word. He feels extremely nauseous after his recital and just wants to flee the quarters and his sadistic superior.

Caesar grinned menacingly and Jack felt like an ensnared animal, trapped and coerced to perform tasks against his will. The Captain's coarse growl was deafening.

"Boy, you must learn my Code perfectly; no excuses and you must obey it wholeheartedly, but just one more thing before you go. Something has been brought to my attention which mightily displeases me... Meadows tells me that yesterday you stole food from the kitchen without permission. Boy, is this true? No lies now, explain yourself... The punishment for theft is, in fact, the second Pirate Code rule. Remember? 'Be Smart: Don't Steal From Pirates'"

Jack's heart sank, he was horrified by Meadows' audacious lies and swiftly replied, "No, Sir, I am totally innocent and would never betray your trust. I know the consequences, please believe me!"

Caesar sneered like a vicious animal ready to attack his prey. "I've got my eye on you, boy! So be aware that if you want to live till the morning, know who I am and that with thieves I show no mercy. Now get out of my sight!" Jack was very angry at this accusation, clearly rattled by Meadows' toxic lies and disappointed that they thought he would possibly not be truthful, capable of betraying him like so many had previously.

As Jack hastily exited Caesar's quarters he realised that in Meadows he had an archenemy who was intent on destroying his reputation and endangering his very existence. He was under no illusion that his only hope of survival was to escape *The Aquila* and its grim and dangerous band of cutthroat pirates. He visualised Salvatore as he lay dying and remembered his last wish for Jack: he would find the lost treasure and use it to make something of his life; in fact he hoped this would give him the strength and resilience to keep going in the scheme of his life – this was all Jack had in his life to cling on to…

CHAPTER 6

Cádiz

As dawn broke over the Bay of Biscay *The Aquila* was draped in an eerie, ghostly, grey mist. It crawled over the ship in an unrelenting manner, obscuring everything in sight.

It was the first thing Jack was aware of as he clambered onto the deck to take the morning air. It had been a difficult night and he felt unnerved and distressed by his nightmare, so vivid and lucid that he wondered if it was an unpreventable dark omen.

Jack dreamt that he finally made it to the shore of Santorini Island… but just as his bare feet hit the hot golden sand he was violently pulled under the water by the coiled tentacles of a fierce sea creature. Jack thought it was a devil from Poseidon's lair sent to extinguish his young life and deny him his riches. He recalled desperately fighting his way up to the surface but very soon his lungs were filled with salt water and the turquoise ocean greedily claimed Jack for itself.

This very vivid nightmare had Jack recoiling in horror and consequently he wondered if he should abandon Salvatore's legacy and just be content to be Caesar's cabin boy. Jack was a truly superstitious soul so this terrifying vision naturally rocked both his confidence and his resolve.

The previous evening Jack overheard Simpson, the ship's navigator, affirming that they were headed back to the Florida Keys, which was in fact Caesar's headquarters, but presently they were near Spain – he was tantalisingly close to his treasure – but how would he disembark and look for it? He realised that although Caesar was a ruthless cutthroat and murderous villain he was indeed better as an ally than an enemy, and so as he sat on deck he made a momentous decision, one that would undoubtedly bring him his heart's desire or exacerbate his downfall. He would risk his future in confiding in Caesar about the treasure of Santorini and engage his interest, of course fuelled by greed and avarice.

Jack had a deep feeling of trepidation but managed to compose himself, get dressed and go below deck. The brutish Meadows soon appeared like an evil dark spectre and Jack knew instinctively that the day's proceedings would no doubt be difficult and unforgiving.

He viciously growled, "Caesar orders you to the sick bay now!" He grimaced with an air of twisted satisfaction as he revealed the gory details of Jack's duty for the day ahead. "You are to assist with Palmer's amputation and clean up the filthy mess!"

The ship's map-reader, James Smith, had unfortunately developed gangrene on his left leg and this had to be removed immediately in order to save his life. Meadows' barked words did not register with Jack at first as he was still shaken by his nightmare, but when the brute kicked open the door with such violent force Jack was startled back to reality.

As he approached the sick bay the putrid stench of acrid blood and rotting flesh was a vile assault to his senses. He could only contemplate what horrors lay behind the door of this grim and foreboding place.

As he turned the tarnished brass handle he felt very nauseous and just wanted to flee, but he realised that whatever hardships he had to endure now, he had the strength to endure it. After all, he always felt Salvatore's presence that was always reassuring… like a guardian angel. Now Jack just had to focus on the future. He resolved to be positive and resilient. He had all to play for with the attractive prospect of treasure and so his time on *The Aquila* was temporary and transient.

Jack meets the ship's surgeon, a portly Irishman named William Flanagan, an educated rogue who was invaluable to the Captain as a capable doctor who had a high success rate of keeping men alive, despite under very difficult circumstances. Caesar was fully aware of his frequent nefarious practice of selling excess medical supplies such as laudanum and opiates to the crew for his own monetary gain. He turned a blind eye to this as he kept the crew numbers at a manageable level, and that's all that mattered to the Captain.

Flanagan sees Jack and immediately instructs him to pick up the discarded bloodstained bandages scattered on the dusty, splintered, wooden floor below the operating table, wash them and then scrub the entire area clean. Indeed, Jack thought this would be no mean feat. His duties completed, Jack is then ordered to the operating table to assist with Palmer's imminent amputation, a particularly gruesome procedure but often commonplace on pirate ships. Jack proceeds to pour whiskey into the unfortunate patient's mouth while Flanagan secures his arms and legs with rope ready for his gangrenous left leg to be detached with his surgeon's saw. Jack feels nauseous and light-headed as this butcher of a surgeon saws Palmer's leg off just below the knee, and as he feels the cold, crimson blood spurt onto his face he is mortified, just wishing to immediately flee the gory scene. *The Aquila* suddenly starts rocking violently from side to side, the ropes securing the patient loosen and the severed limb falls and rolls into the corner of the dingy room. Both men are very unsteady on their feet and a frustrated Flanagan tells Jack to incinerate it in the burner immediately. He didn't need to be told twice and it took all Jack's strength and fortitude to ferry the rotting dismembered limb to the furnace. As he watched the putrid flesh burn and smoke he decided that he could no longer bear this vile barbarism any longer. He would choose his moment carefully that evening and visit Caesar to reveal all about his Santorini treasure; it was a risk worth taking – he could no longer endure the extreme hardships on *The Aquila*. He had the unenviable task of persuading the black-hearted brigand that it was to his financial advantage to help him, his future and no doubt he was about to entrust a man notorious for his lack of mercy and ruthless disregard for justice – it would seem too high a price for most individuals, but Jack was now compelled to show his hand in the card game of life. Flanagan tells Jack to leave the sick bay but remain on standby, as it was very likely his services would be needed again that day. Subsequently, the young treasure-seeker gladly exited the gruesome nightmare of the sick bay... even scrubbing the deck was a welcome prospect in contrast to this vile butchery. He was careful to sneak stealthily down into *The Aquila*'s hulk where his hammock was such a welcome sight. As he rested there temporarily he drifted into an almost meditative state, trying to imagine how Santorini Island would look. His elation at witnessing its precious treasure cascaded and unfurled in his imagination like a majestic carpet of gold and brilliant jewels. He could almost touch it... it had become that vivid in his turbulent mind.

It wasn't long before Flanagan orders Meadows to fetch a reluctant Jack back to the deeply oppressive atmosphere of his operating room. This angered him as he was more focused on consulting with the Captain about his audacious treasure plan.

Flanagan ordered Jack further strenuous cleaning duties, even insisting he revisit the surgery floor, which Jack felt was really pushing him to his already frayed limits. Flanagan's incessant chatter about the previous night's dramatic events on *The Aquila* increasingly irritated him, so through gritted teeth Jack did his best to seem interested and engaged. Apparently, three crewmembers had been struck by lightning the previous day and their burnt, charred bodies were laid out unceremoniously in the sick bay. Jack noticed that, now present, was Flanagan's controversial assistant surgeon, Richard Townsend, who appeared intoxicated and of a very nervous disposition – definitely not the usual attributes of a trustworthy and competent surgeon. Jack felt frustrated that he was compellingly embroiled in this nefarious nightmare; nonetheless, he listened to all the gory details from an animated Flanagan. Apparently, the men died instantly after a lightning bolt shattered the top of the main mast of *The Aquila* and acted as a conductor, in fact issuing a most sulphurous stench as it reacted with the human flesh of the unfortunate crewmembers. It appeared that many men were knocked down suffering burnt arms and legs and it was a miracle that there were not many more fatalities. Jack himself realised that at the exact time of this horrific incident he had been busy cleaning in Caesar's quarters and felt fortunate to have swerved such a violent and excruciating death.

Flanagan smirked as he spoke about the fact that, miraculously, the crewman who had been at the very top of the shattered mast had survived without even a single scorched hair. Jack was then aghast when Flanagan's mood turned intense and dark and he proclaimed that when he informed Caesar about the tragedy the Captain was adamant that the lightning strike was no accident but a bad omen. He believed that one of the men must have cursed *The Aquila* and, consequently, when his identity was revealed he would be fed to the sharks as a terrifying warning to the other men to never dabble in the dark arts on *The Aquila*. It was clearly a crime punishable by death. The Captain was clearly a deeply superstitious man, being of African descent and being familiar with the spirit world, and was extremely temperamental and unpredictable. Despite his deep misgivings about confiding in and trusting the ruthless King of Pirates, Jack was determined to choose an opportune moment and risk all in courting his help to find the Santorini treasure; it was a risk he was willing to take, and so he would be patient till the time was right. Still deep in thought,

Flanagan throws the sick bay keys at a startled Jack and tells him to lock up securely as he rushes out. Jack is suddenly aware of an eerie presence and, from the corner of his eye, he sees the lifeless corpses. He daren't look upon the full horror of the deeply gruesome scene so instead he turns his attention to the round porthole window at the back of the sick bay – possibly the gateway to his freedom and his elusive treasure – he would extricate himself from this tangled web and build a better life for himself. He felt as if the universe was testing his strength and ability to withstand almost insurmountable obstacles, but he hoped, with Caesar's assistance, he would be victorious in his endeavours.

That evening by a real stroke of luck Jack was summoned to Caesar's quarters and, as he exuberantly rushed there, he hoped that the Captain would be in favour of facilitating his treasure expedition.

Caesar is in an unusually good mood and Jack is encouraged when he is praised both for successfully enduring and being effective in dealing with the gruesome horror of the sick bay in light of the fact that most of the crew, irrespective of their rank, had failed to last a day and begged to return to their normal duties. The high-spirited Captain produces a small black bottle of rum with curious gold decoration and slams it on his antique oak desk.

Laughing, he exclaims, "Boy, it takes a real man with strong constitution and courage to be with

Flanagan! Have a good drink tonight, you have impressed me for now. Look lively!" As Jack departs, his hands triumphantly clutching the small glass bottle, the Captain suddenly calls him back and speaks in a decidedly stern tone. "Look, I'm trusting you, boy, OK?" Keep this to yourself: in a few days we are setting off for Cádiz, the Spanish port city. I have important business there and the crew will go ashore and have their leisure time, no doubt to include women and drink; as long as they stay out of jail, it's no concern of mine. You will not indulge with them but will attend me and be a lookout and, of course, this will be a real position of trust, so be warned: any attempt to flee or betray me will be punishable by 'key-holing' without negotiation or mercy. Just keep your head down and be dutiful and all will be well!"

The Captain then walks towards a bemused Jack, peering right into his terrified eyes.

He cackles loudly, "You know, boy, I always see you admiring my jewellery, especially my rings; you know my collection is from all four corners of the world, unique and precious mementos of my travels...

With that, Caesar removes his ornate cygnet ring from his left hand and firmly places it in Jack's hand. He examines it and is impressed by its intricate excellence. It is finely fashioned in gold and jade in the form of a beautiful dragon. Caesar informs a proud Jack that his gift is one of his most treasured possessions, and he was gifting it to him for two reasons: firstly, he felt he deserved to have it and, secondly, it would definitely generate the wrath and envy of other men. So it seemed to Jack that, although he was flattered to receive such a precious jewel, he realised that the Captain was playing a game in which he would monitor the wrath of the crew against Jack being particularly favoured..

Caesar then orders Jack to leave. "Go, boy; prepare yourself for Cádiz and remember discretion is key. I expect your complete respect and obedience at all times!"

As Jack heads back to the ship's hulk to start his covert preparation for Cádiz he is fired up with the increased flames of hope. He would take advantage of his detachment when away from the rest of the hostel crew and reveal his treasure plan to Caesar when the conditions were favourable. His positivity was suddenly dashed by the evil spectre of Meadows who pushed past him with such force that he fell to the ground violently. As he lay on the sunburnt deck he sees the blurred image of Robert Simpson, a trustworthy crew member and, in fact, the unofficial boxing and combat trainer on *The Aquila*.

As he pulled the dazed Jack to his feet he very covertly muttered in his ear, "Don't worry, lad, this week I'm going to teach you how to defend yourself against that wicked brute; we have all endured enough of his toxic behaviour and I'm going to clip the wings of that monstrous brute once and for all!"

Jack felt really pleased and honoured that during the voyage to Cádiz he was now presented with the precious opportunity to be taught self-defence by the best fighter, so skilled and adept in combat that he would finally be able to stand up to the poison that was Meadows. Maybe Lady Luck was finally smiling on his turbulent young life and the thought of finally defeating the vilest of bullies certainly enthused him with a steely determination. To finally defeat his relentless and evil adversary so that he would never again have to endure his vicious bullying was a very attractive outcome for him.

On the one hand, Jack felt honoured that the Captain had unexpectedly gifted him his most precious possession but, on the other hand, he realised that by insisting that he wear the ornate jewellery every day the Captain had a more sinister and twisted motive. He knew that the sight of the ring would ignite the wrath of the crew and its value would make him a target just as much as a valuable piece was worth murdering Jack in cold blood.

As he lay in his dusty, yellow, threadbare hammock contemplating the day, the young treasure-seeker felt unnerved as if a tidal wave of precarious danger was about to drown him. In desperation, Jack considered creeping out in the dead of night to procure a longboat to make his audacious escape, but he knew in reality he was sure to get caught and be executed as a stark warning to the other men to never attempt to escape. It was always best to retain loyalty and respect for the Captain and his beloved ship. After all, tomorrow they would set off for Cádiz and it would be in this beautiful port city that Jack would finally present his treasure plan to his Captain and court the collaboration of one of the most notorious and treacherous of pirates. He was hoping that the prospect of grasping even more wealth would tempt Caesar enough to facilitate his expedition.

Jack's weary eyes finally closed shut and he drifted off to sleep back into the realm of Morpheus. He was in a very vulnerable and powerless position; he hoped his destiny would be as a brave and victorious African lion and not the ensnared deer he felt he was, to eventually be devoured by the murderous villain that was Captain Henri Caesar.

Very early the next morning, the crew were busy preparing for their Spanish expedition and, as Jack perused his long list of duties in Caesar's quarters, while the Captain slept he felt tentative and pressured but he knew that Cádiz could prove to be his gateway to freedom and prosperity. He had the very arduous and responsible task of counting and noting every piece of the Captain's treasure and carefully recording it in a secret journal which only Caesar and Jack had knowledge of. The young treasure-seeker had been party to frequent evening conversations with the Captain when, after a few jugs of rum, he confided in Jack some startling facts and arrangements he had made pertaining to his substantial wealth that he had amassed during his prolific and extremely lucrative career as a very successful pirate.

Jack was still contemplating how he could complete his complex tasks in the least possible time to avoid Caesar's wrath when he heard the heavy thundering thud of lightning footsteps, accelerating to Caesar's domain, and he suddenly felt frozen with trepidation. Jack felt an icy wave of chills ascending his spine; his young heart raced uncontrollably and a succession of droplets of perspiration cascaded down his ashen face. His breathing became frantic and heavy as he noticed the tarnished brass handle of Caesar's quarters turning and his young eyes frantically darted around the ship like an ensnared animal about to be attacked.

It was a total relief for Jack when his surprise visitor was in fact Robert Simpson, his friend, the ship's navigator and unofficial boxing trainer, who bound in with his usual jocular and friendly demeanour. He really couldn't endure another brutal psychological and physical assault from brutish Meadows.

Simpson informed a delighted Jack that their

first boxing lesson would take part in the ship's hulk that evening and that Caesar had been informed and given his consent for Jack to learn the art of combat; he articulated that this would be very advantageous to himself both financially – Caesar would pay him extra spots from the loot for his services and, professionally – as he would finally gain recognition for all the training sessions he had taught over the years on *The Aquila* and other pirate vessels.

The journey to Cádiz lasted some four days and nights and it was reassuring amongst the crew that everyone felt immensely relieved to be venturing ashore. The restrictive conditions on *The Aquila* always presented both complex physical and mental challenges for each man and, as a few had unfortunately succumbed to the fever, the shore time would allow the medical staff to access new medical supplies and water, and have each man take a medical with the Cádiz doctor to verify that they were physically fit for service.

Jack's boxing combat training had exceeded all his expectations and, although his training had been just under a week in duration, Simpson had skilfully transformed the nervous, scrawny young lad into a confident and formidable warrior. He was even developing biceps, a fact that had not gone unnoticed with Caesar who teased the youngster tremendously with Simpson. They both had a real respect and almost brotherly camaraderie with Jack. Meadows had, of course, noticed this development and consequently resented Jack's presence even more, but now with Simpson on Jack's side even he realised that he could no longer openly abuse Jack with violence. For now the young treasure-seeker had a reprieve, but Jack was keen to embark on his treasure-seeking expedition, finally extricating himself from the potential pitfalls and dangers on *The Aquila*. He would be forever grateful for the opportunities that had been bestowed on him, but it was definitely time for him to break away from his present situation and start his own solo adventure... definitely time to forge his own path.

That evening Caesar gave permission for the men to share a few jugs of rum and indulge in the singing of some sea shanties. Jack always found the music and the men's renditions of the ancient seafaring songs a very welcome distraction. Jack had memorised his favourite song and the lyrics he always found particularly endearing and inspiring. This song was entitled 'A Pirate's Life for Me', which was particularly relevant and poignant for himself. He was timid by nature but he always sang the sea shanties with a very animated exuberance, which in fact particularly amused Captain Caesar:

A Pirate's Life for Me

All ye brigands, fallen sailors and robbers on the high seas
Ye decided long ago it's a pirate's life for me...
Conquering, plundering and terrorising your victims,
ensnaring them mercilessly with no chance to flee
Sailing the murky turquoise depths of the high seas
A very skilled mariner crew imbued with devilish panache
Slashing and killing all those poor souls who stand
between them and their treasure stash
So be ye a brave thief of the oceans who isn't afraid to die
Take your chances as a pirate, it's brave but brutal for
sure, that's no lie
'Tis a unique legacy to live in the moment but pay
the price of, to languish in hell
It's a pirate's life for me, the black heart of a
brigand that nobody could quell.

The men enjoyed the interlude of merriment immensely as it gave them a rare opportunity to bond with each other, forget their differences and detach their minds from the harsh realities of the daily existence on *The Aquila*.

The following morning as Jack leaned precariously over the stern of *The Aquila*, peering studiously through Caesar's ornate golden telescope, he suddenly spied Cádiz. The jewel of the Iberian Peninsula appeared almost out of nowhere, rising majestically above the dazzling turquoise ocean. Jack dashed excitedly to the Captain's quarters and informed him that they would soon arrive in that mysterious medieval port.

The big man, still weary from his slumber, snapped back at him, "Boy, me tired; it's only just sunrise! Tell Meadows to take the crew ashore with their supplies and we will follow on later; he knows where the rooms are for the men... we stayed here before. I've decided that you, Farnham and Latham will remain on *The Aquila* with me until all my affairs are in order and I decide when to go ashore, OK?" Farnham and Latham were an inseparable pair of ruthless scoundrels who were apparently notorious in London for street robbery and living off proceeds of prostitution. "And they have been informed of that. Boy, be very careful to curb your tongue and protect my business, OK? Much is at stake in Spain and I want all my plans to go smoothly with a positive conclusion. So I hope its crystal clear, boy. So tend to my things well and mark well that from this day forward I'm bestowing on your young shoulders the ultimate honour. You are to visit my treasure room and only *you* are to be aware of this: the keys are here on my desk; it's your responsibility to check again every piece of my treasure, and I'm trusting you to not acquire any stray piece of glitter for yourself... you know exactly what your fate will be if you walk the wrong path of betrayal. I don't need to say any more!" With that, the Captain's jet-black eyes threw Jack an intensely icy gaze that made him shiver. Jack was dismayed that Caesar was pressurising him unnecessarily to recount his wealth as he had completed the task during the voyage to Spain extremely adequately. He decided that once they were settled on shore in the Cádiz house he would reveal his own treasure plan to Caesar. He had been patient enough; he felt stifled by his lack of freedom on *The Aquila* and so he resolved to strike out on his own. Whatever it took he felt compelled to extricate himself from the Captain's confining control.

Jack felt a deep sense of relief when Caesar finally retired to his slumber, allowing him to clear his clouded young mind and feel more confident and balanced for the difficult tasks ahead.

He likened the glorious ship to an unrelenting and unpredictable jungle where danger lurked in every corner. To survive the many pitfalls he resolved to be like the noble and stealthy black panther, a creature very adept at creeping through the jungle, always on high alert and repelling any lurking beasts who were ready to attack at any given moment.

The Treasure Room was very exclusive indeed and, after a long and arduous four hours, Jack's treasure task was completed and Caesar's precious ledger he concealed carefully inside his shirt. He would of course be extra guarded, and as long as he kept the circling beasts at bay, all should go according to plan.

Jack was already accustomed to having his pistol and Fabio's precious silver dagger concealed on his person every minute of every day. As the vile apparition that was Meadows appeared, Jack informed him of Caesar's precise instructions; suffice to say he trembled with restless rage that just exacerbated his envy and muted his malice towards the Captain's favoured confidant. Consequently, he would disappear out of plain sight on *The Aquila* and conceal himself in the cradle of the ship's hulk. He knew every inch of the ship by now and so would wait it out till he could safely disembark with the Captain.

It was dusk before Jack heard the heavy thud of the longboats being pulled down into the water and, as he crept carefully onto the deck, he could just make out Meadows and the rest of the crew busily loading the supplies, rather like a swarm of industrious soldier ants determined to complete their mission.

Jack was very much relieved when he eventually spied the heavily laden boats with the dreaded brute Meadows at the helm, barking orders for the weary men to row faster. Cádiz port was now visible, its many buildings glinting in the sunlight, beckoning those who were adventurous enough to venture to its mysterious shores.

Without Meadows' relentless tyranny Jack felt newfound positivity and he clutched the Treasure Room keys and headed for Caesar's quarters at around midnight. As he knocked tentatively on Caesar's door it suddenly flew open and there Captain Henri Caesar stood, regaled in his best flamboyant finery. Jack could clearly see that he meant business. He ordered Jack to locate Farnham and Latham and start loading the many treasure chests and trunks containing his most prized possessions. For the first time on his difficult descent into piracy on *The Aquila* Jack felt excited and hopeful. As the steady stream of adrenalin raced through his body he felt newly energised and exhilarated. Cádiz he felt would be the start of a new destiny for him, one that would hopefully lead to his emancipation and prosperity. *The Aquila* had suddenly become a quiet almost eerie place Jack thought, and the very dubious Farnham and Latham who were complicit with Meadows and his nefarious activities never spoke a single word. As they loaded Caesar's precious belongings onto the deck in preparation for their arrival in Cádiz they just fixed an icy gaze of deep disdain on Jack; the evil Meadows had clearly polluted their minds with envy and hatred towards Jack on account of his very close and trusted relationship with Caesar.

Jack was decidedly relieved when Caesar appeared suddenly with a debonair flourish; he was dressed lavishly in his best finery, no doubt to impress and make the best impression on his duplicitous Spanish host... the Captain.

That very evening the shadowy silhouette of the Cádiz shoreline was just about visible to Jack as he surveyed all he could from the deck of *The Aquila*.

As dawn broke the next morning Cádiz port appeared – 'the jewel of the Iberian Peninsula' – rising majestically above the dazzling turquoise waters. Jack hastened himself with renewed exhilaration to Caesar's quarters and informed the Captain that they had arrived in the mysterious medieval port city.

The big man snapped, "Me busy, boy! Tell Meadows to take the crew ashore with plenty supply in the longboats. We will follow on later with Farnham and Latham and I will inform you three when I am ready to go ashore." With that, Caesar threw a set of heavy brass keys at a startled Jack and retorts animatedly, "Count my treasure, boy; be careful to record it in my journal." The Captain points in the direction of an ornate black and gold leatherbound book and glares menacingly at the petrified young lad. The Captain walks away exclaiming in his customary deep tone, "Wake me up at midnight and from hence I will decide when we leave for the shore... don't just stand there; make haste!"

Jack felt honoured but deeply apprehensive about the increasing responsibility bestowed on him... in fact, being the guardian of Caesar's wealth would no doubt ignite further envy and contempt for Jack and he was fully aware that certain nefarious crewmembers would not think twice about sabotage. He knew the young boy would always be looking over his shoulder in a perpetual state of anxiety – an innocent boy now immersed in a perilous pit of venomous vipers.

After informing Meadows of the Captain's very specific instructions, Jack tentatively made his way to the Treasure Room and, with all due vigilance, thoroughly checked he was not being followed or that there was no scoundrel concealed in the shadows lying in wait to plunder and no doubt accuse him of the audacious theft.

It was as day turned into night that the hazy violet glow of dusk descended on *The Aquila* that Jack finally emerged from the Treasure Room decidedly wearied from the arduous hours of counting and recording the Captain's spoils.

It was with a great sense of relief that Jack watched the rest of the crew industriously pack the longboats with sufficient supplies and, as they disappeared on the horizon towards Cádiz, Jack was suddenly confronted by the unnerving hostility of both Farnham and Latham. Jack had been informed that the Captain's treasure would be transported ashore and housed in the residence of the Mayor of Cádiz, one distinguished gentleman named Manuel Mendoza.

With the Captain's precious treasure loaded in the remaining longboats, Jack waits with a nervous but excited anticipation in managing to divert the unwanted attention of the despicable rogues. They made it clear to Jack with their dagger looks and cruel and cutting remarks that they hated him. Caesar, in all his finery, is decked out to the nines and suddenly appears with his customary flourish. This is actually a real relief to Jack, and when the Captain orders Farnham and Latham to go ahead he feels pleased as perhaps now he could reveal his treasure plan to the Captain as he would be escorting him personally; he therefore has a rare opportunity to have the Captain's undivided attention. He knew this was a truly golden opportunity. He was optimistic that after so much hardship and conflict the wheel of fortune could possibly be turning in his favour. He hoped Cádiz would be a transitional and lucky destination for him.

Caesar stands majestically on his magnificent ship and exclaims with his customary loud bellow, "I hope for such a scrawny little boy you find the strength of a lion to row us both to Cádiz!" The Captain finds his remark particularly amusing and his deep laughter rings out with deep resonance in the pitch-black air.

Caesar darts away suddenly like a sleek black panther with business to finish in the jungle; Jack knew instinctively that he was in fact checking *The Aquila* for any corrupt crew hiding in the shadows intent on treacherous mischief, including the ultimate pirate crimes of mutiny and betrayal.

Jack was always aware of how extremely ruthless

his Captain was and that his punishment for betrayal, theft and disrespect was so extreme. During his time on *The Aquila* he had witnessed two men being forced to walk the plank and then to be mercilessly thrown into the shark-infested ocean never to be seen again. Caesar had confided in Jack that he was constantly aware that betrayal and sabotaging plots were always a danger to captains. So far nobody had been that audacious to try to dethrone him; alas, he did not rule out the possibility of this happening one day.

Jack recalled the Captain's very words on his perception of his crew – he reiterated, "This pirate life is indeed cutthroat! You must remember three key rules, boy: 1) Trust only yourself, 2) Sleep with one eye open, and 3) In your heart expect that one day mutiny will darken your door!"

With Farnham and Latham in place, each in a longboat stacked with numerous treasure chests fully secured and meticulously checked, Captain Caesar jumped into the third boat behind them strategically to guard his wealth while they all journeyed the short distance to Cádiz port. As Jack settled in with Caesar and grasped the splintered wooden oars, he smiled to himself as he realised how astute a villain his mentor really was. From their clear vantage point any attempt at theft would be immediately extinguished; the numerous pistols strapped to the Captain's body would be fully utilised to send these two disloyal scoundrels to the depths of Davy Jones' locker, and the many sharks that constantly visited these waters would turn the ocean to crimson without mercy.

Jack rowed with as much vigour as he could muster and, as the lavishly regaled Captain snoozed, his stocky frame sprawled unceremoniously across one end of the rickety longboat.

As they finally reached the magnificent shores of Cádiz, Jack could just about see two shadowy figures waiting in the distance.

As they got closer the Captain suddenly leapt to his feet and, upon spotting their mystery welcome party, growled excitedly, "Boy, I'm so glad we've reached Cádiz. The Mayor, namely Manuel Mendoza, and his devoted son, Ricardo, are my very loyal and gracious friends and business associates! I heard the eldest son and heir, Sebastian, is visiting soon and I have much to discuss with all of the Mendoza family. It pleases me immensely that over the years we have all become the best of friends."

As the longboats arrived laden with the Captain's treasure escorted by Farnham and Latham and carefully guided by an ever-vigilant Jack, the Mayor and his son exuberantly rushed over to instruct his men to assist and Jack was immediately struck by how familiar with each other the Mayor and Caesar seemed. They shook hands and vocalised how happy they were to be reunited once more.

Caesar informed Jack that they would be staying as guests of Mayor Mendoza in the lavish pirates' house and that they should load the treasure chests in the armoury and that he was in charge of the keys. He also told Jack that he would summon him in the evening to instruct him in his Cádiz duties.

As he followed Mendoza's men, working extremely industriously like soldier ants marching at speed to the magnificent house, Jack felt it was a real revelation that his Captain was so manipulative and cunning that he even managed to acquire such government dignitaries and aristocrats in his back pocket, no doubt rewarding them with gold and jewels in exchange for their silence and discretion.

Jack marvelled at the Captain's Spanish pirate house... in fact, he wondered if Caesar actually now owned it. This would make complete sense as the Captain needed a lair and discreet hideaway in Europe; Spain was perfectly positioned on the pirate's map to provide that very facility.

The young treasure seeker felt that the house had a deeply eerie atmosphere and that its depths held many secrets. He was inquisitive and resolved to find out the history of this magnificent Spanish house... and indeed why his Captain viewed Cádiz as a trusted place where he could reside unquestioned and carry out his dubious business affairs, secure in the knowledge that he would not be investigated.

Mendoza's staff were certainly efficient and reliable as it took them no time to load the numerous heavy treasure chests into the armoury which was on the very top floor adjacent to the Captain's rooms. Jack himself was informed that his sleeping quarters would be there, strategically positioned to guard Caesar's wealth day and night. It was clear that the Captain trusted no living soul, but he considered Jack a loyal crewmember. It was to Jack's advantage now that he would have more time exclusively with the Captain in order to finally reveal his plan to find the Santorini treasure; he believed he risked everything in confiding in one of the most ruthless and murderous villains that sailed the high seas – he figured it was a risk worth taking as he could honour the old priest, Fabio's, wish for him to be wealthy beyond his wildest dreams and, in that, Jack found great solace, pride and resolve.

Later that evening Caesar unexpectedly summoned Jack to his bed-chamber. The Captain seemed unusually jovial and animated and, clutching his ornate silver rum tankard, Jack was struck by his almost frivolous demeanour; his stone black eyes twinkled and his devilish smile lit up his battle-scarred face.

He boomed, "You see, boy, I am the most clever of pirates! I have power and influence across all the oceans. Nobody is going to defeat me; I am the King of the Pirates! I rule by fear and I fear no man!"

As the Captain was in such high spirits Jack decided to seize his moment to boldly utter, "Sir, you are the best of pirates and I am very lucky to serve you. I must speak boldly now as I need your help for my own cause."

The murderous villain slams down his rum and at first glares at Jack with deep disdain. Jack continues with gritty determination despite his underlying trepidation.

"Please, Sir, may I speak? I have to fulfil my legacy and as it involves finding treasure on an island I hoped you could help me."

The Captain's eyes light up suddenly and he growls, "So, boy, where is the map for your treasure you talk about? If you are lying and wasting my precious time I will kill you!"

Jack is startled by Caesar's ferocity and he nervously utters, "No, Sir, it's the truth. I would never lie and disrespect you and the map is in my head as I figured it was safer that way. I just need your help to find the treasure; sorry to be so bold."

Caesar cackles with laughter and exclaims, "For such a rakish little boy you have some courage to ask me this. As you served me well and have not betrayed me, so far I will help you to find your treasure. I will send you with Ricardo, son of the Mayor and a few of his men, so that your flag will be on the Spanish government side to enable you to go directly to

Santorini, the Greek island, undetected. You will leave in two days and bring all the Santorini treasure back here. I am attending my business here in Cádiz and so I will await your return. I will also give you Pablo, Mendoza's pet monkey; he will serve as a good lookout and a loyal pet. Please make sure you look after him. He is for sure a lucky talisman. Now go; our business is finished! Leave me to my thoughts and my rum… to the morn!"

The next day an invigorated Jack was duly summoned to the Captain's quarters and, as he entered the sumptuous rooms of Cádiz House, he was immediately struck by the Captain's deep resonating laughter intertwined with another man's voice of Spanish dialect. His curiosity was duly satiated when Caesar formally introduced him to Ricardo Mendoza, the ruthless and very ambitious youngest son of the Mayor.

Ricardo was arrogant and dismissive – having been indulged and spoiled by his parents from a very young age – and looked at a tentative Jack with icy disdain.

He addressed Jack eventually and barked, "You have been instructed by your Captain about our trip to Santorini in two days' time to find the treasure which you state is buried there. It must be clear that I expect obedience and respect from you at all times, and never forget your place! This evening, Caesar and myself will be partaking of a private card game at the Raven and the Moon Tavern at the quayside and your duty will be to serve us and stay vigilant. I hope that's crystal clear!"

"Of course, Sir, I am always your loyal subject. My Captain is always my first priority and therefore I extend that loyalty to your family."

That evening as Jack meandered his way through the cobbled backstreets of Cádiz he suddenly spied in the hazy shadows a weather-beaten wooden sign suspended precariously on rusty chains; the faded image of the blackbird and the full moon were visible but, strangely, the gold letters of the tavern's name were bright and beckoning – *Il Cuervo y la Luna*. As Jack entered he was aghast at the scene he encountered… Definitely decadent and not for those of a nervous disposition.

The tavern was notorious for entertaining dubious characters that facilitated their drinking, gambling and womanising. Jack positioned himself at one of the heavy oak tables and could hardly breathe due to the heavy smoke and the putrid aroma of rum and ale. The place was heaving with vagabonds and women of the night looking to ensnare the men and relieve them of their wallets and gold, amongst other things. Jack was still absorbing the full decadence of the tavern when, suddenly, Caesar enters accompanied by the devious Ricardo Mendoza. Robert Simpson, his trusted navigator and dynamic boxing trainer and the familiar presence of Jean Claude Lavalier. He was the son of a well-respected Parisian aristocrat but had squandered his inheritance on gambling, women and any other decadent activity that he could avail in the dubious drinking dens of Europe.

As Jack waited apprehensively in the dimly lit corner of the entrance a swarthy-looking dark-skinned man approached him and introduced himself as Sinan, the proprietor of all he surveyed. He explained to Jack that he was of Turkish origin, from Istanbul, and had come to Cádiz with his wife and baby daughter, Isabella, 12 years ago. They had set up the tavern with an inheritance of gold from his father and explained that, sadly, his wife passed away some 11 years ago; consequently he had raised his beautiful daughter alone. Sinan further informed Jack that Henri Caesar had already explained that Jack would be meeting him there and that he should be provided with any assistance and courtesy he required. Jack thanked the gracious landlord and, out of the shadows, his beautiful daughter appeared; her beauty was breath-taking. Her mysterious dark brown eyes shone like diamonds and her luscious black curls cascaded to her waist. Jack was mesmerised by her natural beauty. She glanced at Jack shyly, being careful to avert his gaze, and she busied herself cleaning tables, collecting spilt rum jugs, broken plates and discarded food. The customers at the Raven and the Moon were a raucous and decadent band of brigands and Jack felt one such delicate rose seemed very out of place in such a vile pit of vipers. His quiet contemplation was abruptly and surreptitiously invaded by the very animated entrance of his Captain and Ricardo, a man so devious and ruthless that he was capable of any atrocity to serve his ends, and who – it was said – would never accept that his elder brother, Sebastian, would inherit all his father's titles and wealth on Manuel's death. Jack knew that his own life would be in deep jeopardy if he opposed or failed to comply with Ricardo's every demand.

The pirates favoured a fast paced version of the card game bezique in Cádiz and, as Sinan put the final touches to their gamblers' corner, the four players, namely Captain Henri Caesar, Ricardo Mendoza, Jean Claude Lavalier and Robert Simpson, sat in excited anticipation in two pairs around the very ornate and intricately carved oak tables. Jack sat directly behind Caesar with his supply of gold coins. In fact, the stakes were always high; the games were frequently intense and often fraught with real danger. One such testament to this was a grisly skeleton hand, which was displayed behind the bar. Sinan explained that it was an old Spanish custom to decapitate the cheating hand of any player as a deterrent... it seems one such unfortunate was a Moroccan sailor who had been caught cheating and paid a very high price indeed for his audacious misdemeanour.

Jack could hardly breathe through the veil of black

cigar smoke and acrid stench of ale and Caribbean rum and was very relieved when midnight struck and Caesar indicated that he had lost his last game to the French rapscallion, Lavalier, much to his displeasure and thus was ending his evening of decadence. Jack was soon scurrying after him in the depths of the night, the black velvet bags of gold coins weighing heavily in his pockets. Once they arrived back at the Spanish house Caesar told a weary Jack that the Spanish royal family would be visiting Cádiz in their spectacular golden carriage the following day and that he would be excused from his duties to attend the parade through the streets. He was careful to ask his young right-hand man to be vigilant and to report to him in the depths of the night anything dubious or untoward that had occurred in the day's grand celebration.

Jack awoke abruptly as the dazzling sunlight cascaded upon his glowing face.

The house was a positive hive of activity awash with Caesar's busy staff scurrying around like frantic, flustered mice, making preparations for a lavish evening feast to honour the arrival of his Highness King Juan Carlos, her Majesty Queen Gabriella and their young daughters, Princesses Violetta and Giselle.

Before Jack left the Spanish house that afternoon to enjoy the royal parade in the crowded throng of intense celebrations, he meticulously checked and laid out Caesar's magnificent wardrobe; he would wear his finest velvet suit, a rich emerald green creation, decorated with intricate golden thread and ornate brass buttons. His peacock-plumed black leather hat would complete his suitably flamboyant attire and Jack made sure that his boots gleamed and his jewellery impressed. The Captain always made bold statements with respect to his debonair appearance and he always trusted Jack to facilitate this.

Cádiz was in the full throng of anticipated excitement; the imminent arrival of the royal family was, without doubt, always a deep honour for the residents. As Jack joined the animated crowd he surveyed that the narrow, grey granite cobbled streets were flooded with dancing, music and festivities and that the revellers were clad in brightly coloured and ornate costumes with waving flags adorned with the Spanish royal family's insignia.

Jack was positioned at a good vantage point at the front of the crowds who lined the streets. He was still in a daze of disbelief when suddenly the royal fanfare could be heard signalling the royal family's imminent arrival and, before he knew it, Jack glimpsed the mesmerising sight of the magnificent gilded gold carriage drawn by two sleek and glossy black horses. The young lad managed to jostle his way to the front of the crowd and swayed unsteadily in the throng.

He felt so excitable as the royal family rode past and he managed to catch a glimpse of the two princesses. Without warning, he spotted a very ornately pretty handkerchief flutter unceremoniously onto the rough cobbles below. In a moment of sheer spontaneous chivalry, Jack totally forgot himself and dashed to retrieve the delicate piece of linen, boldly returning it to the carriage.

The young Princess Violetta suddenly noticed Jack and exclaimed, "Oh, how kind; this boy fetched my handkerchief," and with that he placed it firmly back in her delicate little hand.

The royal guards acted swiftly and violently dragged a startled Jack away from the royal entourage and brutally struck him several times on his back with a large wooden club. He fell to his knees and writhed in agony. When a horrified Violetta witnessed this she sped along screaming and insisted that the carriage stop. Her parents and sister dismissed her protestations and were very angry that she would lower herself to assist a rough streetboy of very dubious disposition.

Jack managed to break free from the brutal guards who restrained him and he hid carefully out of plain sight, crouching down in a dirty and dimly lit alleyway. Later, undetected, he returned to the safety of the Captain's lair, feeling satisfied and secure in the knowledge that, irrespective of the consequences and potential risk to his liberty, he had respected and served his royal family as only a dutiful and upstanding citizen knows how.

CHAPTER 7

Santorini Island

The Aquila indeed was a truly magnificent and robust ship, having endured many bloody and devastating battles. Captain Henri Caesar felt a great affection and attachment to his sturdy vessel that had defied the odds and still provided safe passage and a modicum of comfort to the loyal crew. In light of this it was with a heavy heart that Jack prepared himself to leave Caesar's fold and embark on his own treasure-seeking expedition with Ricardo Mendoza whom he didn't consider to be imbued with any loyalty. It made him feel very uneasy and it perplexed him as to why the Captain had chosen to trust such a hostile and devious associate to oversee this difficult mission.

Jack was hastily summoned that morning for a meeting with Captain Caesar to discuss his imminent departure, to find his treasure and finally fulfil the legacy that the noble priest Salvatore had entrusted to him. As he tentatively entered the Captain's quarters he noticed that Ricardo Mendoza was already there, accompanied by another finely dressed nobleman who was unfamiliar to Jack.

The Captain fixed his icy stare on the young boy who dared to aspire to greater things and he bellowed in his customary deep accent, "Well, boy, your time has come to find this treasure you are so keen to uncover. You will be guided by Ricardo and make sure you obey his every instruction! This fine gentleman is Raphael Martinez who is a loyal and trusted friend of the Mendoza family, the son of one of the most respected and wealthy families in Cádiz. He is a very experienced seafarer and will advise you on how to reach the island of Santorini so you will have all you need. I have commandeered a small boat – they call it a sloop, actually – equipped for your purpose with all supplies and equipment. I have also decided to send Meadows with you to monitor the treasure expedition, and my ship's navigator, Simpson, will guide and advise you accordingly. I hope you will work as a team! And, of course, I expect the secure delivery of the treasure back to Cádiz where I will allow you to take your share as I instructed you. So, if we are all agreed now you are ready to set sail! Be mindful to take direction from Ricardo and Raphael; they are my eyes and ears. I'm sure you understand, boy.".

Ricardo Mendoza viewed Jack with deep disdain and arrogantly announced, "Boy, you have no experience of treasure hunting and I'm sure your navigation skills belie your tender age, therefore you will be instructed by myself. I will not tolerate insolence or refusal to complete your tasks; I'm sure you will show appropriate compliance!"

Raphael Martinez, the best friend of his elder brother Sebastian, looked on with an air of disapproval; much to Ricardo's annoyance he spoke up with his customary confidence.

"Ricardo, you should be aware that it's your brother's express wish that I assist Jack with all the technicalities of such an arduous expedition and so I'll honour that. I think Jack should be treated fairly with all the basic amenities befitting the Captain's loyal cabin boy... Actually, Captain Caesar, what do you think?"

The Captain made a wicked grimace and proceeded to point his bejewelled finger at a startled Jack.

"Look, you must look after this here, boy; after all, he has never betrayed me and he is my precious property! Ricardo and Raphael, I'm telling you both directly to put aside your differences and guard him and my treasure well. Now look lively, you have much to prepare. You will set sail tomorrow after dusk so you can all leave me now... Report to me in the morn, now go! I'm tired and will retire!"

Jack didn't need to be told twice; he hastily darted

out of the Captain's quarters and made straight for the ship's hulk to organise his few belongings in preparation for his imminent departure. He couldn't help thinking that perhaps Ricardo Mendoza planned to kill him as soon as the treasure was retrieved but he figured that Captain Caesar had sent Raphael Martinez along to guard his life and the loot, as he was a man accustomed to betrayal and disloyalty. He had once mentioned to Jack his preference for the elder Mendoza son, Sebastian, on account of the fact that he always respected their father, Mayor Manuel Mendoza more, and he had in fact facilitated the Captain's paperwork in Cádiz on numerous occasions. Jack went to his slumber in the hauntingly ancient cradle of Cadiz House and knew that his treasure hunt in the morning would change his young life irrevocably.

At the first light of dawn, Jack crept carefully past the Captain's quarters and sped swiftly like an eager gazelle towards the harbour to check that the boat promised by Henri Caesar to take himself and the skeleton crew to Santorini was indeed moored in anticipation of their imminent departure.

Jack was reassured that Captain Caesar had kept his word when he spied from afar quite an elaborate black wooden boat, fully laden with supplies and duly guarded by two of Mayor Mendoza's ever-vigilant servants.

As he made his way back to the Captain's house

he sensed a peculiar ghostly presence behind him and glanced back nervously, only to be startled by the apparition of a hooded figure. He recognised the decrepit face immediately, it was Salvatore, the priest who had bequeathed to Jack his precious treasure map. Jack realised at that moment that this ghostly apparition of his noble benefactor was a sure sign that Salvatore was always with him; he felt strengthened by this before his imminent departure for Santorini.

As Jack darted into the ship's hulk to gather his two linen bundles of belongings, he had one last mission to fulfil and that was to retrieve the magnificent silver dagger that the priest, Salvatore, had insisted he own. It was carefully concealed under a loose floorboard under his threadbare hammock; he wasted no time in retrieving the razor-sharp and very deadly weapon. The silver shard of a blade was hastily concealed in Jack's black leather boot in anticipation of betrayal – the very real threat of an ambush was imminent by the sparse crew to steal the precious treasure for themselves.

Meadows then appeared like an ominous dark apparition and tried to intimidate Jack by staring menacingly at him.

He barked, "We leave now, so get to the boat. You have fooled our Captain but I know you're a dishonest boy... Ricardo knows this, too!"

Jack made sure not to make eye contact with this

deeply wicked wretch and flew out of the ship's hulk with his paltry possessions wrapped in a swathe of faded hessian firmly in his arms.

As he approached the beautiful azure waters surrounding the small expedition boat, Jack could now identify all six men who would undertake the unenviable task of retrieving Salvatore's treasure from one of the cluster of caves dotted around Santorini. Captain Caesar had been very honest about the fact that the islands of Greece were notoriously difficult to navigate and required a unique master to conquer them and retrieve Salvatore's magnificent treasure stash. Jack felt proud that, finally, the glimmer of light that flickered to honour the old priest could now burn bright. If his mission was successful he would have elevated himself in life beyond his wildest expectations.

Upon stepping onto the sloop, Jack noticed that, curiously, it had all the hallmarks of the highly sought after *Black Swan*-class sloops that were originally commandeered by the British Navy.

As the six crew members alighted the designated vessel which would deliver them safely onto the beautiful Greek island of Santorini to begin their quest for the treasure, the men were aware that crossing the perilous Aegean Sea would require the highest level of skill and fortitude. Captain Caesar had therefore reiterated that he had never himself journeyed there but the stories retold by fellow pirates painted quite a disturbing and complex picture. They apparently endured numerous violent storms when their ships had suffered severe damage whilst some crewmembers were hurled mercilessly to their deaths, plunging into the murky depths of the Aegean never to be seen again...

As dusk wrapped its grey and mysterious veil around the crew and their outbound ship, the night waves swept them away from Cádiz and their notorious Captain Caesar. They were now all inextricably linked by their quest for the Santorini treasure. In fact, Jack only trusted Raphael Martinez to some degree; he was under no illusion that the rest were inclined to betray and murder him at the mere glimpse of a chest full of cascading jewels.

As ever, Jack felt that his days on the ship stretched like an eternity and so he busied himself cleaning the deck with a coarse brush and pale yellow sugar soap. He was in charge of distributing their meagre daily rations of food and drink consisting of soda bread, dried meat shavings and a very controlled measure of water. The treacherous Ricardo Mendoza of course confiscated the fruit 'supplies' and rum gifted by Captain Caesar to celebrate their anticipated successful treasure mission. Jack was incensed by this audacity but was mindful to conceal his anger and deep disdain.

Jack counted that four long arduous days and nights on the ship had passed and that the men's morale was low and that there was little teamwork in operation, rather a dark atmosphere of mistrust and isolation. Ricardo suddenly exclaimed that he felt a violent storm was rising and that the crew needed to batten down the hatches and prepare for the merciless manifestation of Poseidon's wrath.

Indeed, that evening in the pitch-black, the mighty Aegean Sea suddenly swirled with such violent ferocity that the men, for the first time, actually agreed to work together to survive. The ferocious rain lashed relentlessly at the entire ship and Jack found himself soaked to the bone, clinging precariously onto the rope that was coiled like a serpent around the ship's main mast. Of course, Meadows in his typically callous manner refused to assist; instead he remained in the lower deck together with Ricardo and Raphael. Simpson had battled the violent waves, desperately trying to navigate the ship in anticipation of calmer seas. Due to the extreme nature of the elements the skilled navigator was fully aware that, running directly before the winds was extremely dangerous during such a ferocious storm; the forces at work were immense and, in fact, if waves fell on the stern this could potentially crush the infrastructure. Simpson therefore decided that the prow or the front of the ship was the strongest part. His strategy was to turn into it as much as he could and so he managed to sail at an angle whilst staying as close to the oncoming waves as possible. This continued on until the volatility of the Aegean Sea subsided and they miraculously managed to keep on course for Santorini despite the main sail being damaged quite extensively and parts of the foremast and mizzenmast breaking apart with the relentless rain falling like cascading bullets and destroying everything in its path.

The subsequent days on the depleted sloop were in fact surprisingly bearable for Jack, as a merciful twist of fate had rendered the treacherous Meadows incapacitated with a serious fever. He had been struck down suddenly by a particularly virulent strain of virus that had confined him to the squalor of the ship's lower deck and, of course, the others prayed that they would be spared this excruciating ordeal. Jack recalled watching in horror as his evil persecutor writhed in agony wrapped in a filthy threadbare hammock; his red and swollen eyes had sunk into his sallow blistered skin and his pale emaciated body trembled uncontrollably... Ricardo seemed particularly anxious about the outbreak of this virulent fever onboard the ship and consequently he ordered Simpson, the navigator, to make haste to Santorini as the Aegean had calmed and was adamant that Meadows was no doubt contagious and that he was to stay in isolation, having been given adequate water and food to sustain him till they finally ventured ashore.

Eventually, it was in the soft amber glow of sunrise that he finally squinted his wearisome eyes to make out the magical Santorini; its towering tropical palm trees were distant silhouettes and the glistening turquoise waters unravelled like a watery carpet onwards to the shoreline. Jack wasted no time in alerting Ricardo, Raphael and of course the ever-vigilant Simpson. Meadows' fever had escalated and was in strict isolation below deck, which was in fact much to Jack's advantage. The young treasure seeker felt so elated that he had managed to survive such a violent and unrelenting storm at the heart of the Aegean and that imminently he would embark on his treasure quest. He was aware that the modest ship was not well-equipped with the necessary tools but Captain Caesar had allowed him a few pickaxes, decrepit shovels and swathes of old rope, and had of course ordered at least two very large chests to be loaded onto the sloop. It was extremely apparent to Jack that Henri Caesar expected the spoils to be returned with due haste, irrespective of the danger, hardships and very challenging terrain on Santorini.

Ricardo and Raphael emerged suddenly from their quarters below deck when the ship was approaching the beautiful Greek island and the younger Mendoza brother quizzed Jack with a real intensity about whether he would be able to lead them to the treasure. He was terrifically sceptical about the fact that he claimed to have memorised the map in his head, but Raphael vocalised that he thought this a prudent move considering that a physical map could have been so easily stolen by fellow nefarious pirates.

Ricardo seemed agitated and he paced up and down the main deck growling his orders to Jack and Simpson.

"Now, look here... You must be ready with all the tools and, Jack, you must have a clear route for us to follow as the Captain expects the spoils to be delivered back to him personally as soon as possible. As you are well aware, any diversion from this aim will be met with severe punishment... Just know your place and act accordingly!"

"Sir, I am clear about my duty to Captain Caesar and I would never betray his trust. I am ready to go ashore and find the cave where the treasure is buried," assured Jack.

They finally arrived on the beautiful Greek jewel that was Santorini and, as Jack carried the equipment ashore, he was in awe of how captivating it was. The glistening carpet of golden sand encircled the tall palm trees that seemed to reach up to the heavens and housed a lively collection of tropical birds that chirped their approval incessantly. Jack recalled Salvatore emphasising to him the sheer beauty of the treasure site and, indeed, it far exceeded his expectations. As the men meandered around the series of caves, Jack knew he was looking for the largest that was framed by two evergreen oak trees. When he finally set his bleary eyes on it he felt such excited anticipation. He informed the men that, according to the map, this was exactly where the treasure was buried. Ricardo glanced at him with sceptical disdain but, like Raphael, didn't utter a word. Simpson indicated to Jack that they should prepare the small oil lamps and both of them entered the dusty, dark and ominous cavern, its granite walls sparkling like a blanket of diamonds, and two large black bats swooped dangerously next to them; they were startled and shaken but mercifully managed to swerve the bloodthirsty creatures.

Jack recalled on the map that in the deeper recesses of this cave there would be a wall that depicted a mural decorated with animals – this is where Salvatore told him to dig. Simpson was informed and the men forged ahead, making sure to cover their faces as the putrid stench of sulphur was so overpowering.

Jack suddenly glimpsed in a dank corner recess of the cavern a section of jagged wall and what looked like the faint etching of a pack of dogs. The black ink had been weathered but Jack was hopeful that this was the gateway to the riches. As his pickaxe struck the cold stone Jack felt cold droplets of perspiration cascade down his face; it became apparent to him that this part of the wall produced an echo that was decidedly hollower and in fact deeper than the rest of the cave. Simpson followed his lead and, after an arduous four hours of wielding their tools, they penetrated the hard and unforgiving granite. It was then that they surveyed a smaller cave made from pale white stone. Instinctively, Jack realised that this must contain the treasure stash that Salvatore had bequeathed to him.

All of a sudden the men heard hurried footsteps and were soon flanked by an agitated Ricardo and Raphael who asked Jack how the search was going. Jack was relieved that Raphael was there as he could always deal with and contain Ricardo's controlling and aggressive behaviour. Jack explained that he was very hopeful that this newly found white cave held all of the Santorini treasure.

And so the four men made their way tentatively into the dark, damp and extremely musty cavern. Immediately Jack noticed that there was very little air and an unbearably acrid odour that was already causing them to cough and splutter.

Jack recalled Salvatore mentioning that the treasure chests would be found behind the wings of a bird, which had seemed very enigmatic. As he examined the cold granite walls interspersed with ice particles, he noticed in the far right-hand corner a blue and white etching of a magnificent bird. Its intricate feathers had been drawn using bright indigo ink that was still in evidence. Jack informed the men that he had found the exact location of the riches and proceeded to fire his pickaxe against the stone.

Simpson joined his arduous labour and, as the pieces of dusty grey rock cascaded down, an aperture formed and Jack could just about see the corner of a wooden and metal treasure chest. After all he had experienced, this was a welcome assault to Jack's senses; he expressed to Simpson that he felt this was the elusive Santorini treasure that had never been found, although so many had previously tried but failed to locate it.

It soon became apparent that there were five large treasure Chests. Upon prising them open, Ricardo ordered Jack to count the treasure and record his findings using paper and quill. He recorded 2,000 gold ingots, each weighing at least three pounds, endless layers of gold doubloons and he counted 50,000 shiny gold crowns. He also counted a hundred handfuls of pearls, stunning translucent diamonds, deep green emeralds and rubies of the richest red – a fortune, in fact – Jack was overwhelmed by the realisation that Salvatore had kept his word. All he needed to do now was facilitate its safe transportation back to Cádiz where Captain Caesar would divide the riches and Jack could start his new life of abundance.

Ricardo immediately took charge of the transportation of the heavy oak chests and personally escorted the men back onboard the ship. Jack was instructed not to interfere with the passage back to Cádiz and that he would be allowed to consult with Captain Caesar only when the treasure was counted and his share of the magnificent cascade of riches was granted to him.

The journey back to Cádiz proved to be highly stressful on account of the devilish Meadows, whose life had previously virtually been extinguished, now making a miraculous recovery and wasting no time in resuming his pursuit and persecution of Jack. He would never accept that Jack would soon be a wealthy young man and he was determined to change the Captain's mind; after all, he had been a loyal and devoted crewmember for over nine long years and, as such, felt that *he* was far more deserving of a share of the treasure.

Jack felt that Meadows would always be his nemesis and vile persecutor and was horrified when he learned of the fact that he cheated death... Jack's future was very much reliant on the Captain keeping his word and he kept himself positive and optimistic; he had a steely resolve for survival. When the welcome vision of Cádiz eventually majestically appeared, Jack prepared himself for the Captain and transporting his newly acquired wealth back home to London.

Back in Cádiz, the Captain's house was indeed a hive of activity. Jack was very relieved when he was eventually summoned to discuss his success in uncovering the treasure and subsequent rewards.

Much to Jack's surprise, Caesar had already divided the treasure. He pointed animatedly at two of the heavily laden ornate chests and exclaimed with his customary boom, "Jack you know I'm proud of you, boy! You followed your path well and your heart and now, as I always promised you, you finally have your gold to set out on your own path! You can go with my blessing and I know you have a deep desire to return to London; it's indeed your birthright and so all my resources are at your disposal."

Jack was so elated that the Captain had actually honoured his promise and he thanked him for always believing in him.

"Sir, you are truly noble and I will never forget how you saved me from perishing. Now you have made all my dreams a reality. I guess I'm now a fully fledged pirate!" The Captain laughed animatedly and rushed over to a startled Jack to grab his hand and hold on with a vice-like grip.

He stared straight into his eyes and cackled, "Boy, now I will journey to my harem in the Florida Keys. Perhaps one day our paths will cross once more. It's been interesting to know you. You take care... and just remember: 'Pirates are born to rule'.

Jack was allowed to keep his treasure stash safely in the Captain's quarters and two days later he was bound for London. Robert Simpson who had proved to be an invaluable ally and confidant accompanied him; having sworn an oath to Caesar to safely deliver Jack back to the London Docklands, he would not even contemplate any betrayal for fear of having his life cut short. And so Jack was soon homeward bound to his London life to begin the next prosperous chapter in his young life. He had survived so many brutal and stark episodes but his perpetual resilience and of course unwavering support from Captain Caesar now set him on a different path, one which Priest Salvatore had always prayed he would follow.

With young Jack Gibson bound for England Henri Caesar decided to journey to his notorious harem in the Florida Keys. This was a highly lucrative business for him and he was careful to source only the most beautiful and well-mannered women for his purposes. It was customary for him to collaborate with a man who had such a reputation for his guile and cunning, one such Myles Partington... He resided in Portugal and would frequent the deep recesses of the taverns of Lisbon and Porto to acquire new girls to journey to the Captain's hedonistic harem. He was extremely ruthless in his work and controlled the unfortunate women with promises of money and lucrative introductions with wealthy clients, but the stark reality was very different from the fantasy he presented. Partington was in fact a cold and callous manipulator of the worst kind, devoid of any morality or mercy but pivotal to the Captain's valuable trade in unfortunate women who had very little options open to them but to comply.

CHAPTER 8

Women

Myles Partington could often be seen frequenting the most notorious pirates' den in the Alfama district of Lisbon, namely The Caravel. Even the locals never dared venture into the vicinity anytime of the day or night for fear of the pickpockets, beggars and unfortunate women of the night who intermingled with the pirates and sailors looking for an opportunity to indulge in all their vices – an endless supply of liquor, poker and ladies' favours could be had for a few gold coins and for many men it proved to be their ultimate ruin.

The Caravel was situated on a perpetually winding slope between the magnificent São Jorge Castle and the mighty Tagus River and was a hotbed of nightly decadence and gratuitous nefarious activity.

Partington was an ex-British naval captain who was disgraced and consequently dismissed for selling arms to the pirate crews; he therefore lived in the shadows and showed no remorse for his betrayal, instead profiteering wherever the opportunity arose. He was of English origin but his weathered skin was tanned. He was middle-aged, tall and of muscular build with a shock of wavy silver hair and bright blue, deep set sparkling eyes. He had first encountered Captain Caesar ten years previously around the card tables of The Caravel during a particularly high stakes game where he lost a great deal of money. Consequently, Caesar promised to write off his substantial debt if he found attractive and willing females to work in his harem situated in the Florida Keys, luring them with false promises of abundant gold in exchange for their compliance in the boudoir. In addition, the opportunity to meet wealthy men who could take care of them, ultimately offering them security and the sanctity of marriage to directly escape their desperate and wretched lives were other options. Partington was therefore a very ruthless and cunning manipulator whose only focus was to finally rid himself of the heavy dark cloak of debt that the Captain had placed firmly on his shoulders. He lived in two dingy, dimly lit rooms above The Caravel and always kept his trusty dog, Samson, by his side. He was a huge black dog who was accustomed to snarling aggressively and revealing his razor-sharp teeth. He was constantly at his master's side and proved to be an excellent deterrent against any unscrupulous characters that visited the tavern who had mischievous intent.

Partington had been tasked by Captain Caesar to find new and more refined women to join his notorious harem situated in Biscayne Bay in a lagoon on the Atlantic coast of South Florida. That evening he waited in the shadows at the entrance of The Caravel as the innkeeper had impressed upon him the fact that three new and very beautiful women had been frequenting his establishment; they had expressed an interest in any arrangements which could be to their financial advantage.

The Caravel was always a busy den of iniquity – especially in the evenings – and Partington played a few tense games of beziqiue accompanied by free flowing rum in anticipation of the arrival of the new additions to Captain Caesar's overexpanding harem. In fact, it was on the very stroke of midnight that three beautiful and finely-dressed women sashayed their way through the dense crowd. Having surmised that they were his targets Partington wasted no time in introducing himself to the ladies. The first was a beautiful flaxen-haired beauty of about 22 years. She was very slim and statuesque and Partington was extremely struck by her beauty. She had stunning emerald green eyes and, as she introduced herself as Abigail, he fixated on her beautiful rosebud lips. Partington directed her to a discreet corner of The Caravel reserved by Christiano, the very vivacious innkeeper who of course allowed these introductions to take place on his premises for a lucrative fee. Abigail had a very attentive audience and she recounted that she had left her husband some two months ago in Porto due to his excessive control and violence and his illicit involvement with other women. She stressed to an enthralled Partington that she was looking for an opportunity to secure herself financially and she had heard about him and his link to Captain Caesar from the notorious owner of The Caravel. Abigail was apparently always very strategic and persuasive with men of means and influence and she was well versed in the feminine art of survival. With this in mind she had arranged for Partington to meet her two lady associates; both had expressed a deep interest in joining her on Caesar's harem and they were expected imminently.

Abigail, despite being young and having reached the tender age of 22 after the end of her very tumultuous marriage, was extremely astute and confident and she saw Partington as a man who could facilitate her ambition and forge a more secure and prosperous life for her. As they waited in the heady smoke- and rum-drenched atmosphere of The Caravel, packed to the rafters with decadent nocturnal creatures, Abigail excitedly described her two friends before they arrived. Lavinia was a lively Spanish beauty of about 24 years whose luscious black curls cascaded to her waist and her light brown eyes shone with mischievous glint. Abigail revealed that Lavinia had left her violent husband in Barcelona and had since found employment as a barmaid in the back-street taverns of Lisbon. She stressed to Partington that Lavinia was very charming and that they always captivated men. He smiled animatedly and asked who the second woman was whose acquaintance he would meet that evening. He wasn't disappointed; the description of Helena really captivated his imagination. Abigail explained that she was a very young French/Romani beauty who was of a golden brown complexion with emerald green eyes and of slender build, statuesque for her tender 17 years. She was completely alone in the world as her parents and brother had been ravaged by scarlet fever when she was only 14. She had survived by working tirelessly in the dusty taverns of Lisbon serving customers, dancing, telling fortunes and strategically using her grace and beauty to attract wealthy gentlemen who could potentially be her way out of her impoverished existence.

As Abigail talked animatedly to an enthralled Partington, the sublime visions of the beautiful Lavinia and Helena descended on The Caravel and their decidedly magnetic aura definitely caught the attention of the hotblooded throng of pirates and sailors who were intoxicated, in the heady throes of wild abandon. As the young women meandered their way through the tavern they looked exquisite, regaled in their best lace dresses of pastel shades of soft pink and lavender lilac, their glossy dark locks adorned with intricate intertwined ribbons. They looked like two elegant birds of paradise floating in a sea of deep decadence.

Partington fixed his gaze upon the two new beauties and was immediately struck by how polished they seemed considering their tender years. Although he was mesmerised by their beauty, Partington thought that Captain Caesar would be particularly captivated by Abigail herself, but only time would tell... He informed a very attentive Abigail that, together with his ship's navigator, head boatswain and four crew members, they would set sail at daybreak the next morning for the Florida Keys where Captain Caesar's harem was housed and where he awaited their imminent arrival. He stressed that with a favourable tide and swift winds he hoped to make the journey within a manageable two weeks. He asked them to be ready at the harbour at daybreak for an immediate departure and that he had arranged for a room to be prepared overnight at The Caravel. With that, he swiftly departed into the night.

As the bright glare of the early morning daylight beckoned a new day, the women, together with Partington, were already at the harbour awaiting their adventure to the Atlantic Ocean and beyond. The ship was very well stocked with supplies and vital equipment for the voyage and the crew of four capable men was already in place. Abigail, Lavinia and Helena were under no illusions that their journey would indeed be fraught with danger and uncertainty, but they felt privileged to have been selected by the Captain to join his harem. They hoped to prosper under his prestigious guidance; after all, he was a man with such a formidable reputation and influence and, being women of limited opportunities, they felt compelled to comply.

The journey in fact lasted for exactly two weeks, and fortunately the ship didn't meet any extreme conditions as it sailed through the Azores and onto the Atlantic. The women and the crew had also been afforded a plentiful supply of good food and fresh water and this made their journey to the Florida Keys far more comfortable than any of them had anticipated.

As they embarked the ship, Abigail exclaimed excitedly to Lavinia and Helena, "Well, how exciting that we are finally here, safe and sound! I wonder what Captain Caesar is like in person? Girls, soon we will find out!"

Caesar's harem was in fact discreetly positioned on a lush, green, tropical island in the depths of Florida, and the party made their way to the Captain's house. They were immediately struck by how tranquil the atmosphere was, but abruptly, by contrast, while they were outside they were overpowered by loud music and merriment.

It wasn't long before the formidable sight that was Captain Henri Caesar appeared, in particularly high spirits. As he fixed his steely gaze on the women he seemed particularly transfixed by the sight of Abigail. Partington noticed this and so his instinct had in fact been correct.

The Captain asked Abigail to visit him at his quarters that very evening and she grinned nervously at him, being both excited but at the same time apprehensive.

Caesar had made arrangements for his close comrade and bodyguard, Thomas, to oversee the new women and provide them with elegant clothes and cosmetics from Paris. Like his Captain, Thomas was also very captivated by Abigail's beauty but she felt very uneasy by his attention.

That very evening Lavinia and Helena, beautifully adorned in their new dresses, joined the other women in the grounds of the harem in anticipation of the two pirate crews whose arrival was imminent, and also a renegade crew of ex-British naval officers who were now in the pay of the Captain, their integrity compromised by gold and the dark vices of temptation.

Abigail noticed that Thomas was physically over attentive; she had to push him away on several occasions much to his displeasure. In fact, one of the

Captain's guards witnessed this audacious betrayal of trust and wasted no time in informing the Captain who became enraged – he wanted Abigail for himself.

Consequently, as they entered the Captain's house, a furious Caesar ensnared Thomas. Abigail was terrified and ran into the study, locking the door firmly behind her.

A bloody and violent fight ensued and the Captain charged towards a depleted Thomas, violently thrusting his sword forward in a darting movement. He smiled a wicked grimace as Thomas was caught off-guard and fell to his knees – he plunged his cutlass deep into his heart, mortally wounding him. The Captain realised it was regrettable he had felt compelled to kill his close comrade; after releasing Abigail from his house he summoned Partington. He informed him that in the morning he would be leaving for North Carolina to visit his comrade Blackbeard, one Edward Teach, who had asked for assistance on his famous ship the *Queen Anne's Revenge*.

And so the Captain would depart to help his friend but also process the fact that unfortunately he had murdered one of his closest friends in cold blood over his love for a woman...

CHAPTER 9

Blackbeard and the Queen Annes Revenge

The Golden Age of Piracy was indeed a time of heady decadence on the high seas and one notorious brigand was sure to strike a deep fear in the hearts of the public, that of Edward 'Blackbeard' Teach. Most ruthless pirates of the time were typically very mysterious and elusive and Teach was no exception. He was of English origin and operated for a number of years around the West Indies and the Thirteen Colonies on the Atlantic coast of North America. His early life is not well documented but it's believed that he was born in Bristol in the West Country. It's likely that he had been recruited as a sailor on privateer ships during Queen Anne's War and that he had recreated himself as a ruthless and fearsome pirate; his unique appearance instilled fear into his adversaries and his merciless barbarism shook them to the very core. Teach was ultimately terrifying and intimidating to everyone who crossed his path and he was considered the 'Devil incarnate'. His adversaries were deeply struck by his long unruly black beard which cascaded down to his waist, tied with ribbons and whom lit fuses that apparently smoked and spluttered, creating an eerie fog around him – this proved very effective in deterring any prospective opponents. His all-black attire, heavy pistols strapped across his muscular chest and flamboyant Captain's hat only created a deeper level of terror, considered an evil spectre and bad omen to all crews. His reputation really resonated loudly on the high seas and few men were complicit in challenging such a formidable adversary.

The year was 1718 and the formidable and unstoppable force that was Captain Teach was very much a deep stain on the revered reputation of the British Royal Navy and, consequently, in collaboration with the formidable Governor Alexander Spotswood of Virginia who had been working on behalf of the planters of North Carolina. A British naval force under the command of Captain Robert Maynard had been dispatched to end the black-hearted brigand's reign of terror.

And so the famous battle of Ocracoke between the notorious pirate, Blackbeard, and the highly revered Captain Robert Maynard was undoubtedly one of the most pivotal and significant events of the maritime history of North Carolina. The legendary date in history was the 22nd November 1718 and the consequences of the brutal and bloody battle would significantly alter the course of the Golden Age of Piracy – forever.

It is interesting to note that only months earlier Blackbeard had in fact decided to abandon his bloody and barbaric life but was lured back to the decadence of piracy. It is well documented that, weeks earlier, the brigand that was Edward Teach had struck terror in the American colonies by the audacious blockading of Charleston, South Carolina, by way of a four-ship flotilla in May 1718.

Apparently, Teach travelled up the Atlantic coastline to the North Carolina capital of Bath (now Raleigh) and supposedly pledged to abandon his plunderous ways whilst requesting a king's pardon from the powerful figure Governor Charles Eden.

In a very audacious manner, as soon as Blackbeard had secured his royal pardon, he resumed his life of treachery upon the high seas.

It was still in the year 1718 and the month of August when, near Bermuda, Teach and his cutthroat crew stormed and captured two French ships fully laden with cocoa and sugar. He then returned to the capital of North Carolina with his bandit crew and boldly claimed that he had discovered one of the vessels abandoned at sea and consequently convinced Eden to declare it a wreck and permit the pirates to acquire its contents. It was apparent that, for Teach, redemption was unattainable and his life would be forever inextricably entwined in the murky depths of the pirate ocean... its pitch dark waves would forever envelop his very heart and soul and there he would reside till his ultimate end.

In fact, it was at the height of Blackbeard's reign of terror that Captain Henri Caesar left his own piracy empire to join his notorious crew on the *Queen Anne's Revenge* and was highly respected by Teach. He prospered financially, was soon promoted to Lieutenant and was very effective during their frequent battles.

Consequently, Blackbeard's many nefarious activities had come to the attention of one Colonial Lieutenant Governor of Virginia, Alexander Spotswood in Williamsburg, less than 200 miles to the north as he suspected it was very likely that Teach would utilise North Carolina as a safe haven to plunder Virginia's shipping interests and thus jeopardise its valuable and lucrative tobacco trade. It's interesting to note that Spotswood had no official authority to implement such a mission but he was determined to root out Blackbeard's base on Ocracoke Island to finally defeat and kill the black-hearted brigand who had been such a thorn in his side for so long.

It was this pivotal decision by Spotswood that would ultimately prove to be Blackbeard's demise and would serve as a deterrent to his fellow pirates.

As well as an overland expedition, Spotswood hastily dispatched a British naval force led by the highly respected and greatly revered Royal Naval Lieutenant Robert Maynard.

In fact, Blackbeard who had eluded the authorities for so long, in the end fell victim to a deceptive trap. Maynard commandeered two well-equipped ships, namely the *Ranger* and the *Jane*, and after anchoring off the southern tip of Ocracoke Island the night before, he ordered the crews to directly advance on Blackbeard. On the very morning of November 22nd 1718 by way of unfortunate events, both the *Ranger* and the *Jane* ran aground. Consequently, the treacherous Blackbeard attempted to flee out of the channel, but miraculously, Captain Maynard and his trusty British crew succeeded in extricating the *Jane* and strategically pulled within shouting distance of the pirates. A fierce battle ensued and it was clear that both sides were prepared to die to be victorious. Maynard illustrated this when he allegedly uttered, 'It was not at first salutation that Teach drank damnation to me and my men whom he described as snivelling puppies and stressed he would never give nor take Quarter'.

Maynard mercilessly kept most of his trusted 60 men very well hidden below decks until nightfall in anticipation of the impending battle with the treacherous Teach. It was clear that neither side was prepared to relent and a brutal battle to the death was definitely inevitable.

Meanwhile, aboard the sloop *Blackbeard's Adventure*, Teach had not identified that it was Maynard and the Royal Navy that they were about to engage with. They conversed under cover of night; nevertheless, Blackbeard allegedly cried out with his customary aggressive tone:

'If you will leave us alone, we shall not meddle in your business!'

Maynard, who was in fact a youthful Lieutenant at only 34 years of age at the time, apparently yelled back audaciously, 'No, we are determined! It is *you* we want and we will have you dead or alive!' Hence both crews were resolved to fight to the death and consequently the gauntlet was thrown.

Blackbeard had lost his precious ship the *Queen Anne's Revenge* before his final battle with Maynard and therefore was compelled to rely on his sloop Blackbeard's *Adventure* that was equipped with only ten guns and a sparse crew of only 25.Although Blackbeard's resources were indeed depleted, the formidable dark spectre of Captain Henri Caesar remained in steadfast defiance and with unwavering loyalty.

The subsequent battle was ferocious and, just as Maynard's sloops, namely the *Ranger* and the *Jane* were ready to attack the *Adventure*, she recovered herself and was soon afloat and ready for engagement. Blackbeard attacked the *Ranger* mercilessly, killing 20 of Maynard's loyal soldiers including the sloop's commander. Consequently, the *Ranger* was out of action and could no longer take part in this most notorious of battles.

Maynard, who was strategically positioned in the second sloop, the *Jane*, ferociously sailed like a shark smelling fresh crimson blood towards Blackbeard's *Adventure* and, in fact, had devised a very tactical plan that would lead to his audacious victory and Blackbeard's untimely death and downfall. The Lieutenant concealed most of his 60-man crew below deck on the *Jane*. He had tricked Teach into believing that the ship was almost empty. When the black-hearted pirate boarded with only 14 crew, his fate was actually already sealed from that point forward. Maynard gave a direct signal to his men who quickly attacked Teach's outnumbered crew. The battle was intense in its ferocity and it is well documented in naval history as one of the most brutal and fearsome battles ever fought on the high seas.

The combat between the two Captains involved an extensive variety of weapons including guns, swords and daggers and the exchange was extremely bloody and brutal. Allegedly, Maynard shot Teach at close range and wounded him badly, but at the same time Maynard's sword broke which was an unexpected turn in the conflict. Teach sustained fatal cuts to his neck and throat and, after being stabbed some 20 times, he finally succumbed to his fatal injuries. Blackbeard's crew, without their brave commander, were vanquished easily by Maynard and, in an act of brutal showmanship, Maynard displayed Blackbeard's severed head below the bowsprit of the *Jane* to symbolise his victory in defeating one of the most feared and notorious pirates who had been so notorious during the Golden Age of Piracy.

Blackbeard's close confidant and fellow pirate, Captain Henri Caesar, witnessed his devastating death and only evaded capture as he hid in the shadows in the ship's hold with the only other two survivors. He vowed to be avenged for his comrade's untimely execution and, not knowing if Maynard and his men remained on-board, he prepared himself for a long episode of concealment. He had always sworn allegiance and loyalty to Teach and they had agreed that in the event of defeat he would blow up the ship in a final act of decadent piracy.

CHAPTER 10

Queen Anne's Revenge

The grave and stark realisation of the death of his close comrade, Captain Teach, at the hands of Maynard was devastating for Henri Caesar. His crew of one witnessed his fury and disdain when he snarled viciously, "I will be avenged for Teach; his death will not be for nothing and I will not rest till that British Navy dog is slain!"

The pirate Captains had been loyal friends and devilish comrades, their hearts as black as night and their corrupt souls drenched in an ocean of crimson blood.

Captain Caesar, believing that Maynard and his men had departed the *Adventure*, tentatively emerged from the ship's dusty hold the next evening. Creeping up to the deck shrouded in the dark depths of the evening, there he spied one of Teach's crew hiding in the shadows. He had sustained quite a bloody gash to his forehead but he would help retrieve the precious treasure that Caesar was determined to claim for himself. It was a still, temperate night and the sky was a striking swirl of black intertwined with eerie crimson tones; a cascade of small shining stars scattered across it like luminous diamonds and the majestic full moon shone brightly in all its lustre and splendour.

A few nights before Blackbeard's death he had requested a meeting with Henri Caesar in his quarters. He reiterated that in the event of his capture he would never be executed and stressed to his loyal comrade that he must blow up the *Adventure* with immediate effect. This would deny Maynard taking any of his crew as prisoners and facilitating their inevitable execution by hanging. In fact, Teach only trusted Henri Caesar implicitly and it was a testament to the fact that he also revealed that, before the inevitable destruction of his sloop, he must retrieve the substantial treasure stash concealed under the decrepit wooden floorboards of the ship's hold.

The solitary survivor from Teach's crew was one Thomas Mason, a heavily tattooed English gunner who hailed from London. He was tall and agile and, despite the wounds he sustained, he wasted no time in assisting the Captain in keeping a lookout for Maynard's men – he considered it an honour to serve and was hopeful that a few gold coins would be granted to him when they were safely off the sloop with the treasure successfully acquired.

Under cover of night, Caesar instructed Mason to thoroughly search the sloop's hold and be very thorough in uncovering Blackbeard's precious treasure; in honour of his slain comrade he would carry out his wishes with ruthless and determined zeal and, with Maynard and his crew a perpetual dark spectre around the bay, speed was required to extricate the treasure from the *Adventure* and blow the ship up as Teach had requested.

Although a much respected and deeply feared pirate captain who had earned his status and substantial wealth through sheer strategy and resilience, Henri Caesar was never averse to rolling up his sleeves when required and, in light of this, he instructed Mason as to the most likely location of Blackbeard's priceless treasure.

The notorious Captain made a very effective lookout... he was under no illusion that Maynard was aware that himself and Mason had survived the bloody carnage aboard the *Adventure* and so he would be determined to capture them both and execute them as ruthlessly as he had sent Blackbeard to hell; he planned to also end their lives in this gruesome and gory fashion.

Mason was a very industrious and determined crewmember and he was also extremely angry at the untimely death of Captain Teach. He expressed to Henri Caesar his distress at Maynard's duplicitous disregard for the Pirate Code; and he was very direct in his intentions to be away with the treasure with immediate effect as his master had specifically requested.

It wasn't long before Mason uncovered the six heavy oak chests strategically concealed beneath the *Adventure*'s hold, and he beckoned Captain Caesar over to inspect the contents, which he duly did with lightning speed. Having detached every rusty brass padlock from its lock with the brutal force of his heavy boot, the Captain was transfixed by the glittering cascade of precious gems filling every space in the deep, dark crevices of the wooden treasure chests. He surveyed the delights on offer while smiling his customary wry grin. There before him were layers of bright yellow Spanish gold doubloons; each side of every coin had the distinctively eerie image of a skull imprinted on it. Multiple lustrous strings of pearls were entwined with a glittering mixture of magnificent jewels including fine-cut diamonds, deep green emeralds and stunning blue sapphires that were the colour of the ocean itself. The sixth casket contained an impressive assortment of solid silver candlesticks, ruby- and diamond-encrusted silver goblets and contraband no doubt acquired from the British Navy command including boxes of gunpowder and lead shot as well as a decent arsenal of Spanish pistols and bloodstained cutlasses.

The dark blanket of night facilitated their transportation of the glittering treasure from the *Adventure* and onto a less conspicuous armoured boat moored further down the coastline. This was one that the Captain had carefully prepared, making sure it was out of the view of Maynard and his men who were no doubt still lurking in the vicinity, hell-bent on slaughtering them in as gruesome a fashion as they had murdered Blackbeard. The ever-vigilant Captain Caesar and his loyal and valiant crewmember, Mason, waited until dawn to make their escape. The sunrise was indeed a sight to behold and intensely striking with the sun's bright yellow beams dancing across the sky and colouring the clouds in vibrant hues of orange and pink.

Captain Caesar informed Mason that they would journey back to Cádiz with Blackbeard's treasure and once safely back in Mayor Manuel Mendoza's territory they could evade the murderous Maynard and for a while avoid the dark spectre of death that was a constant threat for all pirates.

CHAPTER 11

The Final Chapter

The Captain set sail for the glittering shores of Cádiz and felt that imminent stealth and speed was imperative to avoid the duplicitous Maynard. He was no doubt still lurking in North Carolina and, being a sharp thorn in the Captain's side, his execution must be imminent, simply for his audacity in slaying his comrade, Teach. The journey in the newly acquired armoured ship would no doubt be both arduous and perilous but the Captain was a very skilled navigator. As was his customary fashion he had been meticulous and thorough in his preparation. They had more than adequate supplies of food and drink as well as medicine and bandages and they each had numerous pistols and cutlasses at their disposal as well as two very powerful cannons. The Captain had been very strategic in his choice of vessel; it was heavily laden with all the necessary weaponry and artillery required to defeat any potential threats, whether from Maynard or any other crews.

The Captain chartered his course carefully and anticipated that by navigating their treasure ship through Boston and across the temperamental Atlantic Ocean to the coast of Portugal and onto Cádiz their sailing time would be faster. Once on the Spanish coast they would be far beyond the far-reaching clutches of Maynard and protected by Mayor Mendoza from the dark spectre of captivity. The heavy oak treasure chests had been stacked in a uniform line with great precision in the lower level of the arms-laden artillery ship and Mason had been extremely meticulous and systematic in guarding the bountiful treasure. He slept every night with one eye open like a slumbering tiger ready to pounce on any audacious intruder who dared to steal Blackbeard's precious treasure.

Captain Caesar was very meticulous and adept at never showing any emotion or confirmation of trust towards his crew. Although Mason had not betrayed him so far he was dubious about his loyalty and consequently compelled him to meticulously count and record every piece of treasure in his presence and make an inventory. The Captain perpetually ruled with an iron fist and he thought that if Mason realised that any betrayal would be met with certain execution he would be less inclined to succumb to temptation.

The voyage to Cádiz was well into its fifth day when the Captain glimpsed in the cold light of dawn the faint silhouette of a ship that appeared to display a distinctive Jolly Roger flag attached to its main mast. He was extremely dismayed by this unwanted spectre as it potentially threatened their safe passage to Cádiz and he knew that himself and Mason would be compelled to fight to the death as they would never relinquish Blackbeard's treasure.

As the formidable pirate ship closed in on their far smaller artillery vessel, the Captain exclaimed animatedly to a startled Mason, "I'm sure you can see the French flag hoisted high upon their mast – so they dare to enter our territory – they will soon learn that there are grave consequences for this audacious behaviour."

In fact, as it transpired, the Captain of the French pirate ship was one Corsair Nicholas DuPont, a very debonair and accomplished naval captain who had been operating for several years under the direction of the French Crown. Captain Caesar and DuPont spied each other from their decks as their vessels moved closer together and both anticipated a bloody exchange.

The Captain indicated to Mason that they must expect an imminent French attack and that they would have a better view of their new adversaries from the hull of their ship, in fact the section known as the cathead.

DuPont was a ruthless strategist and Captain Caesar was totally unaware that he had been instructed by the French Crown to apprehend him in the event of their paths crossing. It transpired that Maynard was in fact in collusion with the French to capture and execute Captain Caesar and, in exchange for cooperation, he had pledged to supply arms and advice on a battle strategy that, for the French, was priceless. DuPont himself found the generous bounty on Caesar's head too substantial to resist and so he was determined to capture him alive and deliver him to Maynard.

The curious sight of DuPont standing on deck and waving a white flag to indicate that they had no intention of attack definitely took Captain Henri Caesar by surprise but he was, of course, suspicious about their true intentions. He instructed Mason to guard the treasure and decided to approach DuPont as he was fully aware that if the French crew boarded their arms ship they would inevitably uncover Blackbeard's treasure and that this scenario must be avoided at all costs.

Once on board DuPont's ship the crew surrounded the Captain but he was a formidable figure and waited with steely resolve for DuPont to appear.

Captain Caesar towered above the French Captain who was of slim build, and as the two men exchanged words the crew appeared mesmerised by this spectacle.

DuPont spoke with his customary broken English but Captain Caesar understood him.

"So, where are you headed with your arms ship? We noticed you on the horizon... We think, like us, you are audacious pirates. Is that correct?"

Caesar remained chillingly silent for a few minutes and then replied evasively, "We are just transporting arms to Europe; I have nothing more to report."

He clearly did not recognise DuPont as their paths had never crossed but he was very curious, he knew most of the pirate crews. He never showed his perplexity and of course maintained his icy stare.

DuPont invited Captain Caesar to his quarters and he complied, but his sense of foreboding was increasing by the minute.

Once inside DuPont's study, Captain Caesar noticed that at least five heavily-armed crew were positioned inside with a few others on guard outside. He remained silent and, as DuPont spoke, he noticed a very elaborate solid gold pocket watch attached to the pocket of his luxurious black velvet coat. Captain Caesar was fixated on the watch and this didn't go unnoticed by DuPont.

By this time Mason had already been overpowered on the arms ship by DuPont's men and they murdered him in cold blood after they had uncovered Blackbeard's treasure.

DuPont continued his deception by exclaiming, "I think you are a noble pirate like myself and, although we are clearly from different lands, you are my brother in plunder." He laughed animatedly but Captain Caesar seemed more focused on the gloriously golden watch, being unusually unfocused and off-guard.

His inquisitiveness about DuPont's precious watch would prove to be his downfall. After such an illustrious career as a notorious and much-feared pirate this indeed seemed like a decidedly unexpected travesty.

DuPont asked Captain Caesar if he would like the precious gold pocket watch as a gift and a gesture of goodwill and the Captain accepted it without hesitation which, in fact, was very out of character for him.

As soon as Captain Caesar had the watch clutched tightly in the palm of his hand, DuPont's crew suddenly encircled him and pushed him onto his knees.

DuPont then proceeded to taunt the ensnared Caesar.

He exclaimed, "I know you are Captain Henri Caesar and I must now reveal that Robert Maynard is my close associate. He was sure that we would come across you... and here you are!"

Captain Caesar was furious at being deceived by the devious DuPont and when two of the French crew attempted to shackle him with heavy chains and a robust neck iron he broke free and tried to jump into the ocean, but he was eventually overpowered and restrained. The Captain was securely locked up in the ship's hold and DuPont informed him that he was being transported back to Williamsburg, Pennsylvania, to stand trial for murder and that Maynard himself would be waiting to receive him personally.

Despite being tricked and captured in such an audacious manner, Captain Caesar still planned to escape once they were back in Pennsylvania. He would never relent to Maynard and would rather die than be incarcerated. Whatever his fate he would always be the formidable pirate that had ruled the high seas during the Golden Age of Piracy.

As Captain Caesar was led away in heavy rusted chains by DuPont and his crew from their ship now docked in Pennsylvania, he glimpsed Maynard who was staring intently into his eyes, but he managed to avert his gaze; he refused to relent or acknowledge his presence, as even whilst staring in the face of death as a ruthless and formidable pirate he would never show fear!

DuPont informed the newly incarcerated Captain that his trial would be imminent, but for now he would be held in solitary confinement in the local government jail.

The conditions were squalid and oppressive and the only dignity afforded a man of such notoriety was a tin bath full of cold water and a chipped bar of Castile soap. The dingy cell was barely eight feet by four and, as Captain Caesar was tall and muscular, he found the cramped conditions very challenging indeed. The dilapidated walls were made from thick grey stone and stained with the blood of the unfortunate souls who had been compelled to languish in such a hellish place. In the place of a window were thick brutal metal bars which gave the impression that the prisoners were in fact no more than caged animals and that any attempt to escape was futile.

The Captain had managed to conceal the ornate silver perfume vial that he wore on a chain around his neck; now this was especially useful as the fragrant oil contained within it helped to mask the putrid stench of his surroundings. This had been a gift from Mayor Manuel Mendoza in Cádiz and, as he reflected on his present predicament, he wondered if he would ever be reunited with him or if his days were numbered and his death imminent.

His spartan bed consisted of a solitary splintered plank of wood which balanced precariously on make shift legs. Of course, there was no mattress or plush velvet cushions befitting a man of his high ranking, but at least he had been given a coarse hessian blanket to wrap around himself at night.

And so Captain Henri Caesar endured a succession of challenging and quite traumatic days and nights incarcerated in his dark, squalid cell. At times, due to lack of nourishment and extreme dehydration, he drifted in and out of consciousness and consequently felt frequently disorientated.

On his more lucid days, the Captain's thoughts drifted back to his childhood and he remembered the trauma of being separated so brutally from his loving parents, Saul and Letitia, at the tender age of 16. He wondered if they had survived and this uncertainty had affected him deeply, so much so, that his brutal life of piracy had served to numb the pain and distract him from the cruel realisation that he had been compelled to survive without his parents. Their cloak of warmth and security had been ripped away from him so suddenly at such a tender age.

On day 14 of his incarceration in the hellish jailhouse, the shadowy figure of the duplicitous DuPont arrived at dawn flanked by two guards. The Captain was taken in chains to the Colonial Courthouse by an ominous-looking black carriage.

The King of Pirates may have endured two long weeks of squalid captivity and arrived at the entrance of the grand Georgian building feeling exhausted and dishevelled, but as he alighted from the carriage he stood upright and was escorted inside with a decidedly defiant demeanour.

The courtroom itself was elegantly decorated in dark crimson teak and there were 12 seats positioned in a semicircle directly facing the judge's platform, with the prisoners' dock on the left-hand side that was guarded by four armed officers.

It was the 21st November in the year 1718, and on that particular day the presiding judge of the Court of Vice Admiralty Courthouse in Colonial Williamsburg was one Judge Nicholas Trott who had issued the death warrant for the Captain. The impression that an actual trial would take place was a travesty as Henri Caesar's fate had already been decided by this notoriously ruthless judge.

The protocol dictated that the provost marshall, who for this trial was Thomas Conyers, would read aloud the contents of the warrant; he did so whilst staring directly at the prisoner.

Captain Henri Caesar was officially charged with multiple counts of piracy resulting in murder, extortion and of the illegal acquisition of the ships and contents belonging to the Admiralty of both the Americas and Great Britain. He was also found guilty of colluding with, bribing and blackmailing corrupt government officials in order to facilitate the accumulation of his wealth and facilitate his illegal life of piracy for many years.

Judge Trott officially asked the Captain if he had any last request before he revealed his execution date. Although Henri Caesar declined to speak the judge seemed extremely unnerved by the fact that the Captain looked him straight in the eye and smiled at him with a defiant grimace. He could not overturn this decision but refused to plead for mercy and would rather die a pirate's death. He thought his legacy would be that he had survived for 42 years in his lifetime and would be remembered as the successful and notorious pirate that he was.

Judge Trott confirmed that Henri Caesar was found guilty and would be executed on the morning of the 22nd of November 1718 and in the designated place outside the courtroom where pirates met their end. He instructed DuPont to return the convicted Captain to his jail cell and return him in the morning for his imminent hanging.

As the Captain was escorted out of the court he glimpsed Robert Maynard who was complicit in both the capture of Teach and now himself. He felt confident that although his fate was sealed and his life would end imminently, his loyal comrades – namely Jack Gibson, Manuel Mendoza and his sons – would be avenged for his death and ensure that Maynard would not live very long to celebrate his luck in ensnaring him and brutally killing Blackbeard.

On the morning of his execution, as the Captain had predicted, a hooded figure who had been informed of his fate a few weeks previously had travelled in disguise to Williamsburg and now concealed himself well amongst the bloodthirsty pack of wolves baying for the Captain's blood.

This was of course Jack Gibson who was devastated

at the prospect of the death of the man who indeed was a ruthless cutthroat but who had entrusted him and rescued him from near death, giving him the golden opportunity to prosper and facilitate his survival in the most desperate of circumstances.

As he witnessed his Captain being led in his shackles to the gallows he vowed to be avenged for his untimely end. He made sure he identified both Maynard and DuPont who were standing at the foot of the gruesome gallows. Jack would always be fiercely loyal to Captain Henri Caesar and would not rest until Maynard and the equally despicable DuPont were slain... He felt duty-bound to secure his Captain's legacy and would be avenged for his untimely death.

Jack had learnt that, like Captain Caesar, he had not predicted as a young boy to have a pirate's life but their fate predicted that they would be part of this brutal and barbaric existence on the high seas where only the most resilient could endure living in a perpetual state of fear and foreboding.

So that day Jack witnessed the death of one of the most ruthless and successful pirates who ever sailed the turquoise oceans during the Golden Age of Piracy. He was forever indebted to the Captain for his loyalty and trust as, without his protection, he would no doubt have perished and would never have found his treasure or been fortunate enough to enjoy an affluent life that was in stark contrast to his impoverished childhood.

Jack vowed that day to focus with a razor-sharp determination on being avenged for his Captain's death. He felt privileged to have known him and would always honour and celebrate the extraordinary life of one of the most notorious and formidable pirates in history...

Printed in Great Britain
by Amazon

48160033R00098